CLAUDE FROLLO

STARR LEWIS

Palmetto Publishing Group
Charleston, SC

Claude Frollo
Copyright © 2020 by Starr Lewis

All rights reserved

First Edition

Printed in the United States

Hardcover 978-1-64111-901-6
paperback 978-1-64111-902-3
eBook 978-1-64111-990-0

PROLOGUE

From birth, I have been fated to a life spent chasing the light while shrouded in darkness. It seemed my God-ordained destiny to grow into a holy man, and to dedicate my life to a mission: to beat back the sinful Gypsies who continue to spread through my beautiful Paris like a disease.

As the child of a Gypsy woman, I knew only my mother and the ways of her people. I barely knew my father - he died of the plague when I was just five years old. This was a true tragedy; from what I have been told, he was a pious, righteous man of God. He loved my mother truly, though he never approved of her ways. He wanted her to be a better example for me and did his absolute best to draw her into the fold. Though she never truly changed, my mother did become familiar with the priests and families who were my father's closest acquaintances.

Often, my mother left me in the sanctuary of the cathedral for hours, alone but for the people who came in occasionally to pray. I didn't know where my mother went in those days - days that turned to nights spent alone, wondering where she was. If people happened to come into the cathedral and see me, they would take pity on me, bringing me to their homes, feeding and sheltering me for the night. These were my favorite nights, in homes that had true warmth and love. I longed for this intimacy with my own mother, but I learned, as young as I was, that my mother had a cold heart and no room for family- no room for me. Still, I pleaded with her time and again not to leave me alone, to take me with her during the days. Every time, she refused.

One day, she finally decided I was old enough to come with her and learn the ways of the Gypsies. That was the night that I witnessed my first Gypsy bonfire. My mother and all of her Gypsy friends sang in a language I did not know and danced around a fire, waving colorful scarves through the air. As a child, I felt an awe and even fear of these customs that I couldn't understand or feel a part of.

I was soon going to learn the truth about the ways of my mother's people. When I did, my feelings hardened into a deep hatred for the Gypsies, and I adopted the church as my true home. My beloved church was the opposite of my mother and her Gypsy tribe. Where the Gypsies were cold, cruel, and dark, the church was pure light and comfort. I understood that I belonged in service to Christ, and that there was no room for Gypsy sinners if my city were to stay dedicated to the Lord. I decided, though it may sound cruel, that I must rid the city of all Gypsies and their witchcraft. If you are willing to hear my story, please let me tell you how I became Claude Frollo.

PART ONE

CHAPTER ONE

My mother was one of the fastest, wisest, and most evil Gypsies in all of France. She would roam the streets day after day, stealing money and picking pockets. Of course, she wouldn't do this alone. She called her tribe of Gypsy women a harem, but in truth they were nothing more than a gang of harlots. They were merciless, and anyone who got drawn in would soon find themselves victimized. My mother, Ethelinda, was the cruelest of them all.

Ethelinda was beautiful, with jet black hair that looked like waves just before a storm, toffee skin, and green eyes that could capture anyone in their gaze. She had a deceptively welcoming smile that drew people in so that they could never guess her true intentions. Like a siren, Ethelinda enticed men and destroyed them. They would be deceived by her stunning good looks and loose behavior, not realizing until it was far too late that she would rob them blind.

Ethelinda danced through the city each day with her harem, waving a feathered tambourine and drawing people in. They would gather around to watch this spectacle, not knowing that it was nothing more than a group of witches whoring around for alms. While the people were entranced by my mother and the other women, Gypsy children would sneak through the crowds, practicing their pickpocketing on the unsuspecting onlookers. When they began to lose the attention of the crowds, the women would run off as if nothing had happened. They met later in the evening at a distant place, where they would divide their spoils and engage in their customary bonfire. My mother was doing this long before I was even born. From what I've been told, it was in this Gypsy sinfulness that Ethelinda met my father.

CHAPTER TWO

Before he met my mother, my father lived in Saint-Denis, a small town just north of Paris. This was the small town where my father, Gaetan, grew up under the strict rule of his parents and the conviction of the Catholic faith. Though my mother never talked of my father after his death, I learned their story through the people of the church who saw all that happened.

Gaetan met Ethelinda in the Cathedral of Saint-Denis while his family was in mass. He was a young man of eighteen, strong from hard work on his parent's farm. He had skin that was darkened by the sun, and kind brown eyes. That day, he was in mass as always with his parents when, suddenly, the doors of the cathedral burst open. Ethelinda came running up the main aisle, shouting "Sanctuary!!!"

A group of guards followed right behind her, trying to capture her because she was an outcast not welcomed in the city. Ethelinda stumbled and fell to the ground. As the guards reached down to seize her, the priest, Father Renault, looked down from the pulpit and shouted "Halt!"

He walked down to where my mother lay on the ground, shielding herself with one arm. She was young, only seventeen years old, and had a look of helplessness and desperation on her face as she looked up at Father Renault. The father gently took her by the arm and helped her to feet. Gaetan watched all this unfold, and as Ethelinda looked around hesitantly, he was amazed by her beauty. As a young man, he had never seen such beauty before, and fell instantly in love with this mysterious creature. Father Renault looked kindly at Ethelinda, then turned to the guards and said simply, "He who is without sin, let him cast the first stone."

The guards' surprise quickly turned into irritation, and one stepped forward. "This *manouche* doesn't belong here; she is to be beaten and sentenced to death for her crimes. That is the law." The people stirred in their seats and whispered among themselves, shocked by the events unfolding the front of them. The priest released Ethelinda's arm and said firmly, "This young woman came into this house of God looking for sanctuary, and I intend to give it to her. In this cathedral, we do not abide by the savage laws that would have you beat and murder another human being". The look on the guard's face became one of anger mingled with genuine confusion as he said to the priest, "It is our duty to arrest their type. They are criminal savages who live at the expense of the citizens. How can you defend her?"

"I defend the lives of people who are in jeopardy as the Lord has called me to do. If you are so intent on taking this woman's life, you will have to kill me first. Know, however, that you will be sinning against heaven and incurring the wrath of God." The priest held the guard's glare with a cool stare. The whole room stilled and waited to see what the guard would do. After a tense moment, he dropped his gaze and shook his head in disgust. "*Allons-y*" he said, and the guards filed out of the cathedral.

In the silence that followed, the priest looked around at the shocked congregation. "Do not worry, all is well now". He turned back to Ethelinda and smiled. "Do not fret, you are safe here. You are one of God's children, and if he accepts you, so do I. Please, have a seat". He ushered her gently to a seat in the pew next to Gaetan, gave her a reassuring pat on the shoulder, then swept up to the altar and continued with his service as if nothing had happened.

CHAPTER THREE

After the final benediction, Father Renault greeted the people as they left the sanctuary. Gaetan lingered outside, hoping to get one more glimpse of Ethelinda. She was the last person to walk out of the cathedral. She stepped hesitantly up to the priest, who reached for her hands. "Tell me your name, daughter."

"I am Ethelinda, Father. Thank you so much for granting me sanctuary, your kindness will certainly not be forgotten."

"My child, you are always welcome here. This place is meant for all people, and to me, you are no different than any of my disciples. I must say, while I mean no disrespect, you are truly the most beautiful creature that I have ever laid eyes on." Ethelinda smiled shyly.

"You are too kind, Father." Ethelinda moved to release Father Renault's hands, but he held fast to her.

"Ethelinda, it is not safe for you to go back on the streets. We must find you a place to stay." Father Renault released Ethelinda and looked around at the remaining members of his congregation who were standing around, casually talking. "These are some of the kindest people I know, and I'm sure there is someone who will welcome you into their home."

Ethelinda hesitated. "Well... you are too kind, but I'm not sure that I would tax the kindness of these people. I couldn't accept their charity."

Gaetan, who was standing nearby with his parents, I walked up to Father

Renault and Ethelinda. He bowed politely and said *"pardonnez-moi,* but I couldn't help but overhear your conversation. Father, my family can offer this *mademoiselle* shelter. She can work for her keep on our farm, doing chores with my mother. We have only a humble cottage, but we can certainly find room for her." Gaetan looked over and gave a warm smile to Ethelinda, who smiled back hesitantly, with suspicion lingering on her face. Father Renault raised his eyebrows in surprise. "I admire your hospitality son, you have a truly kind heart. I must ask, though, is this really alright with your parents? I would not want you to make such an offer without respecting their wishes and getting their approval."

"Father, you have no need for concern. My parents are kind and welcoming, I am sure they"ll take no exception. If the lady wishes, she would be welcome in our home." Both Gaetan and Father Renault looked to Ethelinda. Father Renault said, "Daughter, the choice is yours. If you choose to go with Gaetan, I can guarantee your safety. If you go back on the streets now, however, I don't know that I can protect you. What do you think?"

Ethelinda looked thoughtfully at the priest, then slid her gaze over to Gaetan. "I accept your hospitality, sir," she said with a small smile.

"Excellent," said Father Renault. "I will accompany you to make the proper introductions." Gaetan, Ethelinda, and Father Renault walked away, heading towards the priest's covered wagon. As they walked away, Ethelinda looked back towards the cathedral slyly. In the distance, a Gypsy harem stood watching them walk away. One Gypsy gave a signal to the others, and they smiled wickedly before running off into the late afternoon sun.

CHAPTERFOUR

A t the Frollo family cottage, Gaetan's mother Rosalie was working outside, planting flowers. She looked up and saw Ethelinda, Gaetan, and Father Renault approaching down the road. She yelled for her husband to come outside. "Alphonse, come here! Gaetan is coming with Father Renault and... that girl, the Gypsy from service." Alphonse walked stiffly to the door of the cottage and leaned against the post, watching as the wagon approached. He was an old man – tall and thin, with bad vision. A lifetime of hard labor had made him stiff and slow moving, which was obvious in his every move. He slowly pulled his glasses out of his jacket, put them on, and walked to the fence. Rosalie followed behind him.

"*Bonjour monsieur et madame!*" Father Renault called out as they approached. He slowed the horses and stepped out of the carriage. Rosalie walked up to greet him. "*Bonjour* Father Renault, how can we help you this evening? I certainly hope Gaetan hasn't gotten in any trouble." She looked curiously behind the priest at Gaetan, who helped Ethelinda from the carriage.

"No Rosalie," the priest said patiently. "As a matter of fact, Gaetan helped solve our problem."

Rosalie eyed Ethelinda suspiciously. "I see. And does this 'help' have something to do with this... Gypsy girl?" As she surveyed Ethelinda – from her long, beautiful dark hair to the curvy figure - the distaste was

9

clear on her face. Rather than looking uncomfortable, Ethelinda looked back at Rosalie, caught her eyes and smirked.

"Rosalie," began Father Renault, "as you saw today, I offered this young woman sanctuary when she was certainly in danger of death. I was compelled by the Lord to save her, and she needs a place to stay so she doesn't end up back in the street. Gaetan was kind enough to offer shelter here in your home."

With some irritation in her voice, Rosalie said to the priest, "Father, my son is truly hospitable, but I'm afraid he's made an offer that we cannot accommodate. I haven't any extra room in my home."

"She can have my room, in the *grenier*," Gaetan said as he stepped forward and looked pleadingly at his parents. "Maman, Papa, I apologize for not asking you first, I meant no disrespect. But this innocent young woman was fighting for her life, and I knew in my heart that my Christian duty was to help her." Gaetan saw the conflict in his mother's face, and he stepped up to her. "Maman, you are always saying how you need more help around the house. With Ethelinda here, you will have that much needed assistance. She will work for her stay – she is not asking for charity, merely an opportunity." When Gaetan finished speaking, Alphonse slowly stepped forward and looked closely at his son. He said nothing and only stared at Gaetan. Finally, he said, "Gaetan, your mother and I are proud of you. Your hospitality is a gift that we cannot deny you… the Gypsy girl can stay and work in our home. You can sleep in the barn for the time being."

Gaetan gave a smile and relieved sigh. "Thank you papa." Alphonse gave a small smile and nod in return, then turned and began his slow, stiff walk back toward the cottage. Rosalie looked highly displeased and huffed. "Well, I suppose that's settled."

Father Renault smiled and said "Excellent! Well, with that settled, I must be on my way. Madame Frollo, thank you. Gaetan, Ethelinda, be well." With that, he went back to his wagon and was soon rattling back down the road.

"Alright, so the Gypsy girl stays," said Rosalie, still with a trace of annoyance.

Gaetan said with some exasperation, "Maman, her name is Ethelinda. You needn't keep calling her that." Ethelinda stepped forward and said with another sly smirk, "Madam Frollo, thank you so much for this kindness. I don't know what would have become of me if your wonderful son had not offered your home to me." She smiled up at Gaetan, who looked away with an embarrassed smile.

"Very well," Rosalie said brusquely. "We'll not stand around out here, let us head inside and get settled." With that, she turned and walked briskly toward the cottage. Ethelinda turned to Gaetan with a smile, and they followed Rosalie into the home.

CHAPTERFIVE

That evening, Ethelinda made herself comfortable in Gaetan's room. Despite her misgivings, Rosalie provided her with some clean clothes and blankets for her bed. Gaetan brought up a few candles and placed them around the room, giving it a soft, warm glow. As he turned to leave, Ethelinda stopped him. "Monsieur Gaetan, I cannot tell you how much the hospitality of your family means to me." She looked up into his eyes. "I will not forget your kindness."

Gaetan reached out as if he couldn't control himself, and delicately touched Ethelinda on her cheek. " I'm sorry... I couldn't resist your beauty any longer. It was my pleasure to offer you my home. A lady like you should always be safe and welcome." Ethelinda gave a small smile and looked down bashfully. She looked up again, and as they stared into each other's eyes deeply, the door slammed open suddenly. Gaetan and Ethelinda jolted in surprise. "Gaetan, there you are," Rosalie said as she bustled into the room. "Well, I wanted to inform you both that it is time for dinner, come down now."

"Yes, Maman," Gaetan said. He ushered Ethelinda out of the room behind Rosalie, and they walked into the kitchen, where Alphonse was already seated at the table. He stood as they entered the room and pulled out a chair for Ethelinda. "Here you are my dear," he said kindly as she sat. Rosalie watched him, her eyes narrowed in suspicion. Alphonse saw her look and pulled out a chair for Rosalie. "And for you, *ma cherie.*" Rosalie sat and gave Ethelinda a look of envy.

"Now then", Alphonse said, "would our guest like to say the word of blessing over this meal?" Ethelinda looked uncomfortable and opened her mouth to speak, but before she could say anything, Rosalie jumped in. "Now Alphonse, you know the girl is a Gypsy... what would she know about prayer? Perhaps you should just say the grace dear." She smirked meanly across the table at Ethelinda.

"I suppose so *cherie*, I just wanted Ethelinda to feel a part of our custom – a bit of prayer may have been good for her. Ah well, let's bow are heads." As Alphonse said grace, Rosalie lifted her head slightly and glared at Ethelinda, who felt her gaze. She looked up and winked sneakily at Rosalie before bowing her head once more.

After dinner, Rosalie began clearing the table, and Ethelinda rose to help her. Soon, Gaetan and Alphonse both went to bed, leaving Ethelinda and Rosalie alone for the first time. After a while of working in silence, Rosalie said to Ethelinda, "Well girl, I can see that my son and husband are completely taken in by your innocent act. I know better. You're one of those sneaky tramps who bats her eyelashes and gets her way. There will be none of that here, not while I'm around. I might not have a choice about you being in my home, but I'll be keeping a close watch on you. Don't think you'll be getting away with any thievery and witchcraft while you are here." Ethelinda just looked at Rosalie as she talked. When Rosalie finished, she sauntered over to her with a dangerous smile on her face.

"I understand perfectly. You are a jealous, bitter woman. You view me as a threat, and that's fine. I'm used to petty women like you." Ethelinda leaned very close to Rosalie's face and whispered fiercely, "Now, what you need to understand is this. I may be a Gypsy and an outcast, but I am a guest of your husband and your son, and as such, I will be treated with respect. I suggest you watch how you speak to me." She held Rosalie's gaze until Rosalie looked away. Ethelinda leaned back as if nothing had happened, turned around and walked away. She turned back and looked piercingly at Rosalie. "You had best get used to me Rosalie, I'll be around for quite a while. While I'm here, I'll work to earn my keep. And trust me...

I'll be keeping an eye on you too." She gave a wink and intimidating smile, then turned and went upstairs to her room, calling *"Bonne nuit!"* over her shoulder.

CHAPTER SIX

L ate that night, Gaetan laid in his makeshift bed in the barn. He tossed and turned, but couldn't fall asleep. Every time he closed his eyes, he could only see Ethelinda. He couldn't stop thinking about her beauty, and the fact that she was in his home, in his room, at that moment. When he couldn't stand it any longer, Gaetan got up and made his way quietly into the cottage. He climbed the stairs to his room and creaked the door open slowly. He looked to the bed, hoping to just watch her sleep, but saw that she wasn't there. He carefully stepped further into the room and looked around. He saw Ethelinda sitting in the window-seat, looking out at the countryside. "Ethelinda?" Gaetan said. Ethelinda looked up, startled, but turned her gaze back to the window when she saw that it was only Gaetan. "Oh, hello Gaetan," she said sadly.

"Is something wrong? I hope you're not uncomfortable here," Gaetan said, walking up to stand in front of her.

"Oh no, you're too kind," said Ethelinda, looking at Gaetan and giving a small smile. She looked down, and a tear rolled down her cheek. "Something far greater troubles me. You needn't worry, I'll be alright." She turned away again, but Gaetan stepped forward and gently took her hands in his.

"Please, tell me what troubles you. I hate to see you crying," he said, looking into her face.

Ethelinda sniffed and looked down. "I am a Gypsy, an outcast in this society. I will never have what you have: a home, a place where you belong. My people have been travelers and wanderers in a strange land for as long as I can remember."

Gaetan listened as Ethelinda talked. He thought about her words, then said, "Well, I could never pretend to understand your history. I don't know the ways of the Gypsies, but I know you can't change what you're born into. You are more than just a Gypsy, though. When I look at you, I see a beautiful woman with the whole world before her. You can't change where you come from, but you can choose where you go. And Ethelinda, you can go anywhere." Gaetan reached forward and brushed the tears from Ethelinda's face. She smiled slightly and looked into his eyes. Gaetan leaned forward and kissed her gently on the forehead. "I should be going... you need rest."

As Gaetan stood to leave, Ethelinda also stood and said "Gaetan, wait." He turned and looked back at her. "From the time that we first met, you have never judged me. You are so different than most of the people I've met... I feel like you really see me. Truly, thank you." With that, Ethelinda leaned forward and kissed Gaetan gently on the mouth. They both smiled as they broke apart.

"Good night *ma belle femme*," Gaetan said. He smiled at her one last time, then turned and left the room. Ethelinda smiled to herself, then went back to her seat in the window. Off in the distance, she saw a Gypsy bonfire, the people dancing and celebrating. "I'll be back with you soon," she whispered. With that, she smiled to herself and went to bed, falling fast asleep.

CHAPTERSEVEN

E very morning in Saint-Denis, the town held a public market. People would come early to get the best food, clothes, and other merchandise. Some people came not to buy anything at all, but just to see their friends and gossip. It was more like a festival than a market, with entertainers busking and children running around playing. One vendor, a middle aged man named Émile, sold exotic women's clothing. Émile was a man who nobody really liked – he was always cross and miserly, and it was obvious that he only cared about the money. Still, women were drawn to his tent, which was hung from wall to wall with skirts and dresses in the brightest, most beautiful colors and patterns.

Émile had only one servant working with him in the tent, a Gypsy boy of about eighteen. He was a small boy, with a drawn, hungry look. Nobody knew the boy's name, and Émile called him only "boy" or "Gypsy". He had dark skin and even darker eyes, which he usually kept trained on the ground or whatever task he was doing. Those who got close enough to see his face were shocked by the long, ugly scar that cut down the side of the boy's face from cheek to neck.

One day, Émile was in a particularly vile mood. He had been cheated on an order that had just arrived, and there was nothing that he hated more than losing money. He spent the entire day yelling at his servant, pushing him around and even striking him. The boy hid in the back of the tent, working and hiding his anger. That afternoon, an older woman wandered up to the tent. She kept her face covered with her scarf, but it was clear from her stooped posture and shuffling walk that she was quite frail. Émile, ever the salesman, noticed only the fancy and expensive rings that decorated the woman's hands, and the weight of the rather large coin purse that she carried on her side. "Ah, *bonjour madame!*" He called out in his most charming voice. "What adornments might a lovely lady such as yourself be looking for today?" The woman looked up at him, and though her face was shaded by her scarf, her surprisingly sharp green eyes peered at him. She spoke with a soft, steady voice. "*Bonjour* sir, I am not entirely sure. I am just browsing... for now."

"Well allow me to help you," Émile said, trying to be charming, "I have a brocade in just the color for you."

"Thank you," the woman replied, "but I believe I'll take a look around by myself for now. I will call for you if I need help, or decide to make a purchase here at all." With that, she walked away, heading towards the skirts in the back of the tent. As she browsed, the woman turned and looked around her slowly, as if searching for something specific. She shuffled up to a garment just to the left of where the servant boy was sitting, cleaning items as Émile had instructed. She reached up as if examining the item, and as she did, she lightly nudged the boy. He looked up in irritation, but as they made eye contact, his irritation quickly transformed into surprise. The woman leaned forward and said under her breath, so quietly that the boy could barely hear her, "*Te voi ajuta.*" Hearing his own language, a look of understanding passed over the boy's face. He gave the briefest of smiles and nodded almost imperceptibly. The woman turned around and called out, "Sir, I will have this one."

Émile, who heard her from the front of the tent, came to the back. Looking at the royal blue and white silk skirt the woman had chosen, he said, "Ah, excellent choice madame. I should tell you, this is one of our most expensive pieces – it will cost you quite a price."

"Of course it will, this is a fine piece," the woman said, waving her hand dismissively. "Tell me your price sir, let's get on with it." As the woman reached for her purse, Émile smiled greedily. When she untied the purse, the woman's hand shook, and she dropped it, spilling coins across where she and Émile stood. He eagerly bent down to pick up the francs, putting quite a few in his own pockets instead of the woman's purse. "Oh, I'm terribly sorry!" The woman cried.

While Émile was distracted, she subtly shook a mysterious powder out of the long fold of her sleeve onto the nearby flap of the tent. She whispered a few words unintelligibly, and suddenly the tent went up in flames. Émile looked up in shock and distress as the whole right side of his tent caught fire. He called for the servant boy to come help him save the merchandise, but could not find him anywhere. As the flames continued spreading, he looked around for the old woman, wanting to make sure that she made it out safely, but she was nowhere to be found. As he looked around in panic and confusion, a flaming wooden beam fell from the top of the tent on top of Émile. He screamed in pain, but there was no one there to save him. He died in agony as his tent burned around him.

CHAPTEREIGHT

A short distance down the road, away from the market, the servant boy stood with the woman who had started the fire. She removed her scarf and cloak, and the boy was surprised to see that she was a stunningly beautiful girl around his own age. There was mischief sparkling in her green eyes, and dark hair tumbled down her shoulders. The boy said, "I don't believe I know you, but I can tell that you are one of my people. Thank you for helping me escape that bastard."

"It was my pleasure", the girl said with a smile. "I could not stand to see one of my people treated in that filthy and deplorable way. I am Ethelinda; my tribe has been in Saint-Denis only a short time. Who are you?"

"I am called Vano," the boy replied. "I have not had a tribe in many years – we were separated in Paris long ago. Many of my family were arrested, and some killed before my very eyes. I was subjected to being Émile's servant, but every day I have planned for the day I could make my escape. Because of you, that day is today."

Ethelinda gave a satisfied smile and shook her head. "Speak no more of it, I was glad to do it. If you have nowhere to go, you are welcome to join my tribe. If you continue down this road, you will see a small path leading off the road to our meeting place. Go there, and tell them who you are. They will welcome a new member if they know I sent you."

"Will you not be coming with me?" Vano asked.

"Oh no," Ethelinda replied with a secretive smirk, "I am in the middle of a much bigger project. Let the group know that I will return soon with news." She and Vano parted ways then. Vano headed towards the woods to find the Gypsies and their shelter. Ethelinda, meanwhile, shed the cloak she wore as a disguise, keeping a light scarf to cover her hair and face as she returned to the market.

CHAPTER NINE

Meanwhile, at the Frollo cottage, Rosalie stood in the kitchen alone, preparing vegetables for that evening's meal. The door opened and Alphonse walked in slowly. "Hello *mon cherie*," he said, leaning down and kissing Rosalie on the cheek.

"Eh, Alphonse, you know not to come so close when you've just come from the fields, you smell like manure." Rosalie said sharply. Alphonse just gave a small chuckle and sat at the small kitchen table, lighting a pipe. "Where are Gaetan and Ethelinda?" He asked as he leaned back and blew out a cloud of smoke.

"Against my best judgment, I sent that little Gypsy harlot to the market with my list of things to purchase. I hardly trust her, but she must work for her keep if she is to stay in this home. Gaetan drove her into town, and Lord only knows what he's doing." Rosalie said.

Alphonse gave another low chuckle and said, "With the way he was looking at her last night, I wouldn't be at all surprised if the boy was following her every step around the market." Rosalie suddenly put her knife down and turned to face her husband.

"I don't like this, not even a bit, Alphonse," she began, launching into a full tirade, "this girl is trouble. She may seem innocent and helpless, but I know that it is all an act. Our son has such a kind, gentle heart. This girl will take advantage of him, and if we don't do something, she will break him. She will use her beauty and false delicacy to draw him in, and he is too blinded by her 'charms' to take any caution. We cannot let him be lured into this Gypsy's trap!"

Alphonse calmly released another cloud of smoke before speaking. "Rosalie, I am surprised at you. If you are honest with yourself, you know that this isn't really about protecting Gaetan. You are jealous of this girl – her youth and beauty intimidate you. Honestly, *cherie*, you must correct your pride and do the Christian thing by giving the child a chance. All of this is beneath you."

Furious, Rosalie walked up and snatched the pipe from Alphonse's hand. "Give me this filthy thing," she snapped. "How dare you call me jealous and prideful? I cannot believe that even you won't support me in this. Some day soon, you will see that I am right about this girl. You are just as taken in by her as Gaetan! Well, so be it, but you will both see." Huffing, Rosalie turned and went back to her cooking.

Alphonse rose from his chair and came to stand behind Rosalie. "All I ask, *ma cherie*, is that you give the girl a chance. She may be a Gypsy, but there is good in her. Trust Gaetan's judgment and, more importantly, trust mine."

Rosalie sighed deeply. "For you, *mon coeur*, I will do my best." She put down her knife and food and leaned back against her husband. "I know that Gaetan's heart comes from you, you are a gentle soul just like him. I don't like it, but I trust you." Alphonse said nothing, just wrapped his arms around his wife and held her close. They stayed like that for a long time, just standing together.

CHAPTER TEN

In the days that followed, Ethelinda became a working member of the Frollo family. Although Rosalie was still cold and harsh, she gave her more and more responsibilities around the house. Ethelinda did everything asked of her and never complained, despite the hard work. She was polite and sweet to the Frollo family.

The more time that Gaetan and Ethelinda spent together, the more they found themselves falling for each other. He was curious about all the places that Ethelinda had lived, and felt like he could listen to her talk about these exotic and faraway places for hours. Ethelinda found herself loving his openness and sincere interest in her as a person. She told Gaetan things that she had never told anyone outside of her tribe before. This was new and exciting for her, but also terrifying – she knew that was not what she was there for.

One night later that week, when everyone in the house was asleep, Ethelinda rose from the bed and quietly exited her room. She tipped down the stairs and out of the house, careful not to disturb anyone as she went. She moved quickly and silently, and soon she was running through the wooded land beyond the family's farm. She stopped when she heard the faint sound of tambourines and singing not far ahead of her. Smiling, she walked forward through the trees and approached her harem, who were holding a bonfire in their shelter, which was shielded from public view by the trees and brush. Ethelinda stepped forward into the light of the fire, and one of the Gypsy women looked over and saw her. She smiled wide and exclaimed, "Linda! You've returned!" The others turned and saw Ethelinda. She joined the group, and they embraced before continuing their bonfire. Ethelinda sat between Vano and a young woman about their age, Sophia. "So," Sophia said, turning to look at Ethelinda, "how have things been, Linda? Are you enjoying the glamorous life with your new family?"

Ethelinda smiled coolly at Sophia, her eyes were sharp and edged with irritation. "No dear," she replied, "As a matter of fact," she said, turning to face the whole group, "I'm not sure that this is worth pursuing anymore. I thought when I got caught up with that priest that I would take advantage of the situation, but the Frollo family is a bad target. They barely have anything... I can take what they have, but it won't be a big enough payout. I say we put a curse on the mother, take what we can, and move on." The rest of the Gypsies looked surprised and a bit confused at Ethelinda's sudden change of plan, but nodded their agreement. Only Sophia and Vano still looked suspicious.

"I wonder," said Vano, "why put a curse only on the mother - shouldn't the whole self-righteous, so called Christian family suffer. They are part of the people who have treated us like less than them for so long. I think we should curse the whole family... father and son included."

"Vano," Ethelinda said in a sweet voice, placing her hand on his chest, "you are letting your own emotions impact your judgment. Let me handle this. The only one who has done wrong to me is the mother, and she is the only one I intend to punish." Vano looked into Ethelinda's eyes, sighed, and nodded. "Excellent." Ethelinda said with a victorious smile. "Now, I'll be needing to get back before the family starts to wake. I will return to you all soon – for good." Ethelinda hugged her harem and said goodbye, then darted off, back into the shadowy woods.

CHAPTERELEVEN

The next morning, Gaetan went, as he often did, into town to help Father Renault clean in the cathedral. Gaetan dusted the pews of the sanctuary when he heard Father Renault call out behind him, "Ah Gaetan, and how are you doing? By the time you finish each week, I have the cleanest sanctuary in all of France."

Gaetan smiled and walked up to the father, bending to kiss his ring. "Bless you Father. This is work that I like to do. I must admit, it gives me time to get lost in my thoughts."

"I think I can guess what you're thinking of these days... how is Ethelinda doing? Is she settling in well?" Father Renault looked carefully at Gaetan, waiting to see how he would respond.

Gaetan looked away guiltily, then said, "Can I be perfectly honest with you, Father?"

"Of course you can son, but is this something you would prefer to say in confession?" Father Renault said, looking concerned.

"Oh no, it is nothing like that. The thing is, well, I think I'm falling in love with Ethelinda. I know I'm young, and I want to do what's right before God." Gaetan looked up at the stained glass windows of the cathedral, staring at the scene of Christ hanging on the cross. "I want to do right by everyone. But every time I look at Ethelinda, I forget everything else. All I can think about is her, and being with her. I don't think I've ever had feelings like this before, Father, and I don't know what to do."

"Son," Father Renault said with a calm smile, "there is nothing wrong with the way that you are feeling. I know you, and believe that your intentions are pure. Most importantly, the Lord knows your heart, and He knows that you want to do what is right. That begins, though, by telling Ethelinda the truth about how you feel."

"I don't know Father. After all, she is a Gypsy. That doesn't change anything for me, but

I don't know how she would feel about being with anyone outside of her culture. The last thing

I want is to scare her away – if she runs back to her tribe, I may never see her again."

"Gaetan, you must let go of this fear. God did not give you the spirit of fear. If He wills for you to be with Ethelinda, then that is what will happen. He is always with you… you merely have to listen and trust Him."

Gaetan thanked Father Renault and left, the father's words echoing in his head the whole ride home.

CHAPTER TWELVE

When Gaetan arrived home, he walked into the cottage and saw Ethelinda sitting at

the table, looking lost in thought. Gaetan stood looking at her for a moment, then walked over and said, "Ethelinda, how are you? Is everything alright?"

Ethelinda looked up as he approached and smiled. "Oh nothing is wrong, I'm just thinking. Do you remember what you said to me the first night I came here? You said I can't change where I come from, but I can choose where I go from here. I've been giving that a lot of thought recently. I never really felt like I had a choice, but being here with you makes me think I might. The way that you hold to your faith and believe in your God makes me think there might really be hope for me."

As he listened to her talk, Gaetan realized just how right the priest was. He felt determined to tell Ethelinda the truth of how he felt. "Ethelinda," he began, "I know that God is faithful, and that He loves us no matter what. He is the only one who knows our futures, and everything that happens is for a reason, leading us on our path. I know that God loves me because my path has led me to you."

Ethelinda looked up in surprise and smiled at Gaetan, who continued talking. "What I'm trying to say, Ethelinda, is that I am in love with you. I didn't know what my future held either, but looking at you and being here with you know, I feel for the first time like I really know what I want."

Ethelinda's eyes shone with tears, and she beamed. "Oh, I feel the same way Gaetan. I was afraid, though, that you wouldn't trust me or ever truly feel the same way about a Gypsy girl like me. I love you, and if I truly have a choice in my future, I want to choose you."

"I am so happy to hear you say that, *mon amour*. I know we've only known each other a short time, but this feels right." Gaetan grasped both of her hands in his, bent to the floor on one knee, and said, "Will you marry me Ethelinda?"

Laughing and crying, Ethelinda bent down in front of Gaetan. She looked into his eyes and whispered, "Of course I will." They leaned forward and kissed, then stayed there hugging for a short time.

When they stood up again, Gaetan said "I am so overjoyed! We must tell my parents this news when they return home." He looked at Ethelinda's face and saw that she looked uncertain. "Is something wrong?"

"No of course," Ethelinda assured him hastily. "I love you, and I am ready to marry you any time. I think, though, that perhaps we should wait to tell your parents, springing news like this on them too suddenly could be problematic. They are good people, but we still don't know how they will respond to your choice of marriage to a Gypsy."

"You are right... perhaps we should wait. Tomorrow then. when we all gather in the evening for supper. Then, we can tell them together." Ethelinda smiled, but still looked a bit hesitant. "Don't worry *ma coeur*, my parents might be shocked – especially my mother – but they love me and want what's best for me. Once they understand that you make me happier than I have ever been, I just know they will understand."

"If you say so Gaetan... I believe you." Ethelinda smiled reassuringly and drew Gaetan close. They kissed and hugged once more. "Now," she said, "I must go get everything cleaned up and prepared before your parents come in for supper." With that, she gave one last smile, then turned and went into the kitchen. Gaetan stood with a look of pure tranquility, then turned and went outside for a walk, lost in thoughts and dreams of Ethelinda.

CHAPTER THIRTEEN

T he next morning at breakfast, Ethelinda and Gaetan tried to act normal, as if nothing had changed between them. Rosalie, however, watched them closely, and she could tell that something was different about Gaetan. When she could stand it no longer, she said "Gaetan, I'll be going into town today, and I will need your assistance. Will you accompany me with the wagon?"

"Of course I will, maman, I would be happy to help with your shopping." Gaetan replied pleasantly.

"Well that is an excellent idea," Alphonse said. "My friend Louis is coming to visit with me today, otherwise I would take you into town myself." He turned and looked at Ethelinda. "Perhaps this afternoon, Ethelinda, you will be able to serve Louis and myself some refreshments. How does that sound?"

Ethelinda liked Alphonse – he was quiet, but kind. "It would be my pleasure Monsieur Frollo," she said with a smile. Gaetan couldn't stop himself from smiling as he watched her. Rosalie squinted with suspicion and displeasure when she saw the look on his face, but said nothing.

Later that afternoon, Ethelinda was in the kitchen preparing some refreshments when she heard Alphonse enter with his friend, Louis. Louis was the owner of the nearest farm, and he had known the Frollo family for many years. He was a short, skinny man with dingy clothes and stringy black hair. He wore a thin mustache and goatee and had a crooked smile. He was not a kind man, and had a reputation for being a mean drunk. When he was sober, he was extremely smart, which was why he had so much success with his farm. Nobody really like Louis – not even Alphonse – but they still got together for the occasional card games and to discuss business.

Alphonse and Louis walked into the kitchen, and Alphonse said "*Bonjour* Ethelinda! Allow me to introduce to you my friend, Monsieur Louis Porton. He is the owner of the Porton farm down the road. Louis, this is Ethelinda, she works here in our home with my wife."

"Monsieur Porton, nice to meet you," Ethelinda said with a polite curtsy. As she spoke, Louis looked her up and down lasciviously, his eyes taking in every curve and lingering on her chest before finally looking up into her eyes. He gave a slimy grin and said "Mademoiselle… Ethelinda, was it? I'm sure the pleasure is all mine."

Ethelinda looked annoyed and uncomfortable and said, "Well, if you'll excuse me, Monsieur Frollo, I told Gaetan that I would feed the animals while he is out today. I think I"ll do that now, if you're not needing me for anything."

"No, go ahead. Thank you Ethelinda," Alphonse said. Ethelinda nodded and moved to leave, but before she went, Louis gave a slick bow and said, "Mademoiselle, I do hope our paths cross again." Ethelinda gave a quick, fake smile and curtsy, then brushed past Louis and out the door.

Louis watched her walk out, and Alphonse looked at him suspiciously. "Louis, I'm not sure I like how you were looking at that young girl. I know you've had your troubles in the past with young women, but you are not to cause problems for that girl."

"Oh please," Louis responded dismissively, "do not try pretend you are so high and mighty that you haven't noticed a beauty like that sitting right under your nose. Besides, those Gypsy types are used to a little something *sexuelle*… there's no need to act like you haven't considered having her in your bed." Louis sat back and looked at Alphonse with a smug, knowing smirk on his face.

"Of course, I will admit that she is a beautiful young woman," Alphonse said heatedly, "but how dare you insinuate that I would do such a thing with her – she is practically a child! And Gypsy or not, she deserves more respect than that. You ought to be ashamed of yourself Louis."

Louis leaned forward, his eyes narrowing into slits. "You always did think you were better than me... you and your little prude of a wife. She's old and crusted up just like you, no matter how much you walk around acting like you're important."

Alphonse slammed his hands down on the table, then jolted forward and grabbed Louis by the collar. "You dare come into my house and speak this way about me, and about my wife? You are no longer welcome in my home... Get out, before you get yourself hurt." Alphonse pushed Louis forcefully away from him.

Louis fell to the ground, then staggered to his feet. He gave a shaky laugh, then said "Don't think I'll forget this Alphonse... you've made an enemy now."

"Just get OUT!" Alphonse yelled. Louis glared at him one last time, then slinked out the door. Alphonse, breathing heavily, sat and put his head between his hands.

CHAPTERFOURTEEN

Instead of going home, Louis stood outside, furious and breathing heavily. He looked around, deep in thought, until his eyes landed on the barn. He gave a mischievous smile and slinked towards the barn, where Ethelinda was feeding the horses. He watched her with a lustful look on his face, then stepped inside and said "Hello mademoiselle *Chienne.*" Ethelinda turned, startled, and her eyes narrowed when she saw Louis.

"What are you doing here? Is there something you want?" Ethelinda said suspiciously.

Louis stepped closer, eyeing Ethelinda's cleavage. "Oh… you know exactly what I want. I bet you could tell from the moment I saw you, you turn me on. Look at you – that body, those eyes, that hair." Ethelinda took a step back and tried to turn away, but Louis stepped closer and grabbed her by the arm. "Come on Gypsy *traînée*, don't act modest now. I see you Gypsy women all the time, dancing and whoring around. Don't act like you're all modest now. Give me what I want… I know you want to."

A dangerous look flashed across Ethelinda's face, and then, she smiled seductively. "Show me what you want," she said in a low voice. She slid her shirt down low on her shoulders and stepped closer to Louis.

"That's more like it," he said with a smile, his eyes greedily taking in her body. He leaned forward and kissed her on the neck, then worked his way down, kissing her breasts. Ethelinda gave sighs and sounds of pleasure, then removed her shirt. Louis started playing with her chest, lifting her breasts and licking her nipples. Ethelinda signed and moaned, and Louis said in a low voice, "Yeah, you know you like that. Have you had enough?"

"Not exactly," Ethelinda whispered. She moved her leg between Louis' legs, knee just nudging his penis. He laughed a little, thinking that she was being sexy. As he reached down to undo his pants, Ethelinda jammed her knee up into his groin. As he groaned and doubled over in pain, Ethelinda removed the belt from her skirt and wrapped it around his throat. She put her knee in his back and kept pulling the belt tighter until Louis' neck snapped and he slumped over, dead. As she looked at the body, Ethelinda's eyes held a dangerous fire. She looked at his dead body and spit into the dirt "*Sale porc.*" She glared at the body, then looked around for a place to hide it. She grabbed Louis' body beneath the arms and dragged him to the back of the barn. She threw some hay on top of him, then brushed her hands off, breathing heavily. Ethelinda fixed her clothes, then walked casually out of the barn, heading back to the house.

CHAPTER FIFTEEN

Meanwhile, in town, Rosalie and Gaetan were making rounds to the local shops, picking up their supplies and food. As they walked down the street, Rosalie said, "This is nice, isn't it? It's been so long since we went out, just you and I. Ever since that Gypsy has been staying with us, I feel like I haven't seen you at all."

"Maman, please don't be dramatic. I've enjoyed having Ethelinda around, but you are always important to me." He smiled and kissed her on the cheek, then turned and kept walking.

"All I'm saying, Gaetan, is that I worry about you spending too much time with her. You are my only child, and don't want to see you falling to any bad influences. The Gypsies are trouble!"

Gaetan sighed deeply and turned around. "Maman, we were going to wait and tell you this later, but since you keep bringing her up... I have news for you. I have asked Ethelinda to marry me, and she said yes. We are in love, and I pray that you find it in your heart to be happy for me."

Rosalie stood in shock, and tears filled her eyes. "Take me home," she whispered, then whirled around and walked back to where they had left their wagon. Gaetan looked distressed, but followed his mother to their wagon. On the ride home, Rosalie refused to talk to him, and they rode in icy silence all the way back to the cottage.

When they arrived, Ethelinda was cleaning in the kitchen while Alphonse sat, smoking a pipe. "Hello you two, how was your day?" He said as they walked in. Neither spoke, and Alphonse looked back and forth between them. "Alright, what is going on here? Tell me what happened."

Gaetan stepped forward and said, "Papa, we were going to wait and tell you properly, but... Ethelinda and I are in love, and we have decided to get married." Gaetan went and stood next to Ethelinda, wrapping his arm around her shoulders.

Alphonse looked stunned and said, "And are you both certain of this decision? You've known each other such a short time, do you not think it's too soon?"

"I know all I need to." Gaetan said defensively. "I knew from the moment I met her that I could never feel about anyone the way I do about Ethelinda, and I know now that she feels the same about me. That is all we need."

Alphonse rose and walked to where his son was standing. He looked him in the eye and said, "If you feel so strongly, I imagine there is nothing I could say or do to make you feel differently. I give you my blessing." He shook his son's hand and smiled at Ethelinda, but turned as Rosalie started sobbing.

"How could you!?" She cried. "This Gypsy witch waltzes into our home, and all of a sudden you all are acting as though she belongs here! I cannot allow her to come in here and take my own son away from me!"

"*Cherie-* " Alphonse began, but Rosalie cut him off. "No! For too long, I have been ignored and rebuked for even suggesting that the little Gypsy girl is not all she pretends to be. I refuse to be guilty in my own home any longer – this girl is dangerous, and she will not take my son without a fight." Rosalie strode forward and slapped Ethelinda hard across the face. She reached up to hit her again, but Alphonse grabbed her by the arm and held her back.

Gaetan stepped in front of Ethelinda and examined her face. When he saw that she was alright, he whirled around to face his mother. Anger, hurt and sadness mingled in his eyes. "Clearly, *Maman*, we are not welcome here any longer. If you refuse to accept the woman I love, then you will lose me. We are leaving here as soon as possible." Gaetan grabbed Ethelinda by the hand and they marched out of the house.

As they left, Rosalie began to sob again, turning and burying her head in Alphonse chest. He held her and rocked her back and forth as she cried. After a short time, he said quietly, "Rosalie, do you remember the day I asked your parents for your hand in marriage? Your mother hated me." He said with a low chuckle. "She interrogated me for a whole evening, but it was worth it when she finally said yes, and I could have you as mine."

Rosalie peered up at Alphonse, a small smile playing over her lips as she remembered. "Mother never did like you. When she saw how happy you made me, though, that was all it really took for her to give her blessing."

Alphonse kissed the top of her head. "And I love you just as much today as I did that day, *ma cherie*."

"But you understand why this situation with Gaetan is different, don't you Alphonse? We cannot trust him with a Gypsy. Those people have reputations for the dangerous things that they do to men. If he insists on being with her, I cannot stand to see it. I cannot stand to watch my child be destroyed."

"I understand Rosalie, I do," Alphonse said. "What you have to decide, though, is if that is a good enough reason to lose your son altogether. No matter what we say, he will go and be with Ethelinda, because that is what love does – it gives you no choice but to be with your love."

Rosalie sighed deeply. "I just don't know, Alphonse. I will try, but I just don't know."

PART TWO

CHAPTER SIXTEEN

Meanwhile, Ethelinda and Gaetan sat together in the barn. Gaetan was upset, and after a short time, he spoke. "Ethelinda, I am so sorry for my mother's behavior. I didn't expect her reaction to be quite so extreme... I hoped she would just be happy for me." He looked down sadly.

Ethelinda took one of his hands gently in hers. "Gaetan, no matter how upset she was, your mother loves you. In time, she will accept us because she can't lose you. In the meantime, we will go out and start our life together. I will always be here for you, and I know you will be there for me – you have been from the first day that we met."

Gaetan looked up and stared into Ethelinda's eyes. He saw love and determination in her gaze, and it fortified him. "My dearest, you are right. We belong together, and that is the most important thing. As long as we have each other, we will always have a home."

Ethelinda and Gaetan looked deeply into each other's eyes, feeling closer than ever. They leaned forward and kissed, slow and sweetly. They kept kissing, their breathing getting heavier and more passionate. Gaetan laid Ethelinda gently in the hay, and they made love, unable to resist the temptation any longer.

After the fact, Gaetan and Ethelinda lay on their sides, just looking at each other in contentment. Ethelinda reached forward and placed her hand on Gaetan's chest, just above his heart. She looked in his eyes once more and said softly, "You are my future."

Gaetan smiled. " And you are mine." They leaned forward and kissed once more.

CHAPTER SEVENTEEN

Late that evening, Ethelinda and Gaetan quietly pack all of their belongings in a small wagon. Once everything is packed, Gaetan takes one last look back at his home, and they ride off into the cold, foggy night. As they ride, Gaetan tells Ethelinda, "I know of a place where we can go safely... Friar Joseph Angles, a monk who I met through Father Renault. He lives far off the beaten path, but I am sure he would provide us shelter."

Ethelinda and Gaetan rode on for some time until they finally pulled into a nice, tan house. Gaetan got out of the wagon and said to Ethelinda, "Wait here, I will go talk to Friar Angles." Ethelinda nodded and watched as Gaetan walked up to the front door. He knocked, and soon, a short, chubby man in a nightgown opened the door, rubbing his eyes. He looked startled and said, "Gaetan, is that you?"

"Yes, Friar, it is. I consider it a true blessing that you opened the door."

"Has something happened to your family, Gaetan? What sort of trouble must you be in to come to my door at this unsightly hour?"

"Oh no sir, I assure you it's nothing of that nature. We just needed help, and didn't know where else to go."

"We?" Friar Angles questioned. He looked past Gaetan and saw Ethelinda sitting in the wagon, watching their exchange. He looked back at Gaetan. "Ah. I see... *that* kind of trouble. Well, bring her inside – you both must be freezing."

Gaetan beamed and hugged Friar Angles. "Thank you so much." He smiled at him once more, then went to get Ethelinda and put the wagon and horses away in the stables. He sighed, shook his head, and headed back inside.

When Gaetan and Ethelinda came inside, Friar Angles said to Gaetan, "Well, don't be so rude son, introduce me to the lady!"

"Oh," Gaetan said, "Ethelinda, this is Friar Angles. He is a good friend of Father Renault, and one of the best men I know. Friar, this is Ethelinda, my fiancée."

Friar Angles raised his eyebrows in surprise, but gave a small, polite bow to Ethelinda, who curtsied back. "It is a pleasure to meet you, Ethelinda. Please, won't you both have a seat? I think we may need some tea to get through this night." Ethelinda and Gaetan smiled and sat at the table. Friar Angles returned a short time later with the tea tray. "Help yourselves." He said as he sat the tray down on the table. He then took a seat at the table and looked at Gaetan. "Now then, tell me: what brings you to my home?"

"Well, Friar," Gaetan began carefully, "my fiancée and I need a place to stay until we are married, which we hope to be as soon as possible."

Friar Angles looked at Gaetan skeptically and said, "So what you are saying is that you need a place, and that you would like me to perform the marriage." Gaetan nodded. "Well obviously, you know that I have several questions for you."

"Yes sir, I supposed you might," Gaetan said with a small smile.

"Good then. Do your parents know what you are doing?"

A shadow flickered across Gaetan's face. "Yes they know, though my mother doesn't quite approve."

"I see. And does Father Renault know that you've made this choice, that you're here?" Friar Angles asked. Gaetan looked away guiltily. "So I'll take that as a no." He shook his head in disapproval. "And I suppose you've come to me to marry you? Gaetan, you should know better than that. If Father Renault won't marry you, I certainly cannot."

Gaetan leaned forward, his eyes pleading with the friar. "Please, Friar Angles. Father Renault told me to listen to my judgment and trust the will of God, and I believe He gas led me here. I would have asked for the good father to marry us, but there is no life for me and Ethelinda back home. We came to you so we could be married and rent a room – start our future together."

Ethelinda spoke up suddenly. "Sir, as a Gypsy, I have been met with hatred and prejudice my whole life. I have never belonged anywhere but with my tribe. But when I walked in the cathedral in Saint-Denis, Father Renault saved my life. He treated me like everyone else, and it is because of him that I met the love of my life. We wouldn't do this if it was any disrespect to him, and I know that Gaetan would be no part of it if it wasn't pleasing in the sight of your God. He is the most faithful and dedicated person I have ever known."

Friar Angles looked back and forth between the two young people sitting in front of him. Finally, he sighed deeply and said "Yes, I will help you." He shook his head with a small smile. "I have a feeling if I didn't, you would just find someone else who would."

They all stood, and Gaetan stepped forward and hugged the friar tightly. "Thank you so much," said with excitement, "we will be married in the morning!" Ethelinda smiled and gave another small curtsy.

"Very well then. I don't have any rooms fully made up, but you can both make yourselves comfortable in the first floor rooms. If you both follow me, I'll show you to your rooms." Ethelinda and Gaetan followed Friar Angles, holding hands and grinning excitedly.

CHAPTEREIGHTEEN

I n the wee hours of the morning, when the sun was just beginning to peek over the dark clouds, Gaetan woke in the bed Friar Angles had provided. He looked around, momentarily forgetting that he wasn't at home. He then remembered where he was and why, and he couldn't stop the excited grin from spreading across his face all over again. He rose and dressed, then crept down the corridor to the room the Friar had given Ethelinda. He knocked softly and said, "Ethelinda, it's me."

The door opened, and Ethelinda poked her head out. "It's time, my love," Gaetan said with a smile.

"I am so excited," Ethelinda said, smiling back. "I will be right down." She and Gaetan kissed, and he headed down the hall to meet Friar Angles while Ethelinda finished getting ready.

"Good morning sir," he called as he approached the friar.

"Ah Gaetan, good morning." The priest stood holding his Bible and the vows for the ceremony. Are you ready for this, son?"

"I have never been more excited for anything, Friar."

Friar Angles smiled. "Excellent. And where is…" he trailed off as Ethelinda came down the corridor in her wedding clothes. She didn't have an actual wedding dress, but still looked stunning in a long, dark green dress. It was made of the flowing, magical-looking fabric that the Gypsies were known for, and was embroidered down the skirt with pink flowers and light green leaves. Her hair was tied up into a beignet, with tendrils falling into her face. She smiled as she approached, and asked, "How do I look?"

Gaetan looked in awe and said *"Dieu a envoyé la lumière de ma vie."* His eyes sparkled with tears, "I cannot believe this gift he has given me." Ethelinda smiled at him.

Friar Angles cleared his throat and said pleasantly, "Shall we begin ?" Both Ethelinda and Gaetan nodded. "Excellent. Do you have rings to exchange ?"

Gaetan and Ethelinda looked uncomfortable, and Gaetan said, "Actually... we don't have rings."

"That's quite alright, I figured you might not. I have some for you – consider them my wedding gift to you both." The friar said with a smile. He pulled two simple bands of polished iron out of his pocket. "Before the rings are exchanged, I will bless you both with holy water. Friar Angles picked up a bowl of holy water from the table behind him, then prayed over it. After he prayed, he dipped a ceremonial spoon into the bowl and filled it with water, which he poured over Gaetan and Ethelinda's heads. "Bless you in the name of heaven." After he blessed them, the friar handed Gaetan and Ethelinda the rings. "Gaetan, place the ring on Ethelinda's first three fingers, symbolizing your union first with the holy trinity," he instructed.

Gaetan placed the ring on Ethelinda's thumb, index finger, and middle finger, saying. "In the name of the Father, of the Son, and of the Holy Ghost." Finally, he slid the ring on Ethelinda's ring finger "I marry you, wife." Ethelinda grinned. After she placed the ring on Gaetan's finger, Friar Angles led them through their vows. He prayed once more, then said, "By the power given to me by God, I now pronounce you man and wife." Gaetan grinned and hugged Ethelinda, picking her up and spinning her around. "I suppose this goes without saying... you may now kiss the bride." Friar Angles said with an amused look. Gaetan and Ethelinda kiss.

Later, after their celebration, Gaetan approached the friar in his chamber. "Friar Angles, do you have a moment? I would like to discuss important business with you."

"Yes of course, come in Gaetan," the friar replied, waving him into the room. "What do you need?"

"Well sir, Ethelinda and I appreciate your kindness and hospitality. Thank you for welcoming us into your home. We need a place to stay while we get on our feet, and I would be so grateful if we could stay here. Of course, I would pay you for room and board – once I find a job, that is – and Ethelinda would be willing to work as a housemaid."

"Gaetan, slow down," Friar Angles said reassuringly. "You've only just been married, take a moment to settle into that. You and Ethelinda can stay here as long as you need to, and pay me when you can. For now, you are my guests."

Gaetan sighed in relief. "Thank you good friar. Your kindness to me and my wife will never be forgotten." Gaetan left the room with a smile and went back to celebrating with his new wife.

CHAPTER NINETEEN

By now, I'm sure you are wondering how I fit into this tale. Well, I would like to tell you that things stayed happy for my parents, but the things that I am about to share with you will change this story. Let me tell you how it came to pass.

Ethelinda and Gaetan spent many happy weeks in Friar Angles' home. Gaetan found a job on a nearby farm and made a living for him and Ethelinda. Ethelinda spent a great deal of time with Friar Angles, working in his home and getting to know him. As time passed, though, she felt more and more the call of her people, who were trying to summon her back to her tribe. She tried to ignore the whispered urges for her to return to her home – she was happy with Gaetan, and didn't want to be who she had been anymore.

Late one night as Gaetan slept, Ethelinda laid in bed, unable to sleep. "The spirits are calling me," she said to herself, "and I cannot ignore them any longer." She quietly slid out of the bed and went to the middle of the floor. She knelt and folded in on herself. She inhaled deeply, then rolled her eyes back in her head so that only the whites could be seen. She began whispering and chanting incantations in Romanian. As she whispered, she suddenly disappeared from the room.

When she appeared again, Ethelinda stood just outside of her harem's campsite. She heard them inside the trees, chanting and singing, and she breathed deeply before approaching. As she approached , several of the Gypsies turned and saw her. They started talking amongst themselves. As she stood there, Vano walked up to her. "Well... I'm surprised you finally came back, Ethelinda. We certainly have missed you," he said with a sly smile, "but I suppose you've been too busy with your new little life to miss us." He reached forward and put his arm around Ethelinda, drawing her in for an uncomfortable hug.

"Oh, leave her alone, Vano," said a young Gypsy woman, stepping forward. She looked at Ethelinda and smiled. "Hello, cousin."

Ethelinda squinted at the girl and stepped closer. "Kezia, is that you?" Anyone looking at Kezia and Ethelinda could tell that they were related. Kezia was short and curvy, and where Ethelinda was darker in complexion, Kezia had fair skin. She had wavy, light brown hair. Her eyes, however, were the same startling shade of green as Ethelinda's, and she had the same straight, white smile. Ethelinda looked at her cousin in surprise, then leaned forward. The hugged tightly, and Ethelinda said, "What brings you here? I have not seen you in so long."

Vano stepped forward. "I mean, we had to summon her when we realized you had gone off the deep end with this Frollo person."

Kezia rolled her eyes and gave Vano a look. "Don't mind him," she said dismissively. "In all honesty, my harem had a few close calls in Paris – many of my people have been arrested, and some even killed. I needed a place to come, and I could think of no one better than you." Kezia smiled and squeezed Ethelinda's hand. "That is why I was so surprised when I came here and found that you had not only left the tribe, but had married someone from outside our own kind. Tell me, how did this happen?"

Ethelinda and Kezia sat and talked, and Ethelinda shared her story with her cousin. After she told her story, Kezia said, "So you are happy then?"

"Yes, I truly am. Gaetan is such a gentleman, and he loves me, not even caring about my being a Gypsy."

"I see." Kezia said. "Well, you know that I want you to be happy always my cousin...but you cannot just leave your true family. You are a Gypsy, and you belong with us. What about Gaetan's mother? What have you done about her?"

Ethelinda looked uncomfortable. "Well... nothing yet. I suppose you're right though, this is who I am, and who I always will be. I will put a curse on Rosalie."

Vano interjected. "My goodness, this man has made you soft Ethelinda! That woman treated you like a servant in her house, and she hit you. She and her whole house should be burned alive."

Ethelinda's eyes narrowed to slits as she looked at Vano. "I see what's going on here... this isn't about my revenge at all. You are jealous, aren't you Vano?" He looked away, but Ethelinda gave a mean smile and sauntered up to him. She sat very close and planted a kiss on his cheek. She put her mouth on his ear and whispered, "Don't forget that I am the one who brought you here. I have seen and done things that you couldn't even understand. Leave my husband alone, or you will see a side of me that will haunt your nightmares forever." She leaned back and gave a satisfied smile. "Is that clear?" Vano nodded his head silently, and the other Gypsies looked at Ethelinda with a new respect.

"Now," she said, "as for a curse on Rosalie, I and Kezia will handle that. Kezia, we will go now to her house and place the curse, then you return here to the harem. I will return to my husband." With that, she shot a glare over her shoulder at Vano. Kezia smirked and followed Ethelinda away from the group.

Vano sat glaring angrily into the fire. He muttered angrily and dropped a stick into the fire, causing the flames to leap higher. As he watched the flames rise, he said to the rest of the harem. You all se what is happening here? We are losing Ethelinda to those people... the same ones that persecute us, that treat us like animals. Her curse will not be enough. She will run back to that husband of hers and be lost to us forever." The other Gypsies considered his words and began to nod in agreement. "I say, Ethelinda may start that curse, but we will finish it," Vano said, grinning into the smoke and flames. The other Gypsies laughed and cheered, and they all celebrated their dark plan.

CHAPTER TWENTY

The next morning, Gaetan woke to find that Ethelinda was not in bed with him. He sat up and called out for her. "Ethelinda? Where are you my dear?" From downstairs, he heard Ethelinda say, "I'm down here!" Gaetan rose from bed and went downstairs, where Ethelinda was sitting at the table. He kissed the top of her head as he sat down. "Are you quite alright? You're up so early." As he looked at her, Gaetan noticed something was different about his wife. She had a glow about her, and a look that he couldn't quite place. He searched her face, trying to figure out what it was.

"Well darling… I actually do have something to tell you," Ethelinda said mysteriously.

"What is it?" Gaetan said nervously. "You know you can tell me anything."

"Alright. Here it is – I am with child." Ethelinda smiled nervously, waiting to see how Gaetan would react.

"You mean, we're going to have a baby? Are you sure?" Ethelinda nodded with a slight chuckle. "Yes, I have suspected for some time now, but I didn't know for certain until yesterday. Are you excited my dear?"

"I can barely believe it… this is wonderful!" Gaetan exclaimed. He leaned forward and hugged Ethelinda tightly. As they broke apart, Gaetan had a serious look on his face. "Ethelinda, nothing could make me happier than having a child with you. I think, though, that this is the kind of news I must share with my parents. I have been so happy here with you, but the truth is, I miss them both dearly. I think we need to go home and see them."

Ethelinda looked uncomfortable, remembering what she and Kezia had done to his mother just the night before. It was nothing too serious, they had only plagued her mind with nightmares and terrors. Still, she hesitated at the idea of going back and seeing her again. She loved Gaetan too much to tell him no, though, especially seeing the hope on his face. After a moment of deliberation, she said "You are right. It is time that we go back and make things right with your parents, at least for our child's sake."

Gaetan looked relieved and hugged her tightly once more. "Excellent! I will ready our wagon and tell Friar Angles we are leaving." He kissed Ethelinda, then hurried off, leaving Ethelinda sitting at the table, deep in thought.

CHAPTER TWENTY ONE

Gaetan and Ethelinda rode back towards the Frollo cottage – Gaetan looked eager, but Ethelinda fidgeted nervously. Gaetan could see Ethelinda's discomfort, and he smiled over at her reassuringly and said, "Do not worry, my darling. My mother is bound to come around when she hears our news… we are starting a family!" Ethelinda gave him a small smile, and they continued riding.

As they got closer, Gaetan and Ethelinda saw plumes of black smoke rising above the farm. "What in the world… *Mon Dieu.*" Gaetan said in fear. He sped the horses on, and as they approached, they saw that the cottage was in ruins. Everything had burned down, from the cottage to the stables. The whole area smelled like smoke and burned flesh. "No." Gaetan whispered. He leaped out of the wagon, and Ethelinda followed close behind him. They picked their way through the ruins to the cottage, and Gaetan called out "Maman? Papa?" There was no answer and he stepped further into the rubble. Ethelinda followed carefully, looking around in horror. Dread built in the pit of her stomach and she knew beyond any doubt that this was the work of her tribe, and of one person in particular. "Vano." She whispered.

Gaetan dug in the remains, searching for any sign of his parents. He stopped suddenly, crossing himself as he came across a hand – his mother's hand, almost unrecognizable from burn damage. He jolted up and ran outside, where he vomited. He stood crying, just outside the remains of his home. Ethelinda stood, staring in shock at the hand. She fell to her knees in front of the hand and dug away pieces of rubble, crying as ash fell all over her. She uncovered the body of Rosalie, so badly burned that it was almost impossible to recognize her. "I'm so sorry," she whispered. She reached out and gingerly grabbed the burned hand, placing it on her stomach. "I am sorry that you will not meet your grandchild." She cried quietly, still holding Rosalie's blackened hand. After a short while, she said "Thank you for giving me your precious son, the light of my life. Goodbye, Mama Rosalie." She gently let go of the hand, then rose and went to where Gaetan stood outside. He was sobbing uncontrollably, and Ethelinda walked up and wrapped her arms around him.He turned and sobbed against her shoulder, and she held him, crying silently. They stood that way for a while, and when Gaetan's tears slowed, he sat up and looked at her. His eyes were unfocused, and his voice was ragged as he said, "I must go talk to Father Renault." He turned and walked to their wagon, where he unhitched a horse and rode away down the road. Ethelinda watched him go with concern, holding her stomach. She then turned her gaze and looked towards the wooded path that led to her harem. She squinted, then stepped toward the forest area.

CHAPTER TWENTY TWO

When she arrived at the harem camp, Ethelinda found them all laughing and talking, smoking and having some kind of celebration. Vano looked over and saw her, and gave a slow, dark smile. "Well, look who it is. How is the family Ethelinda?" He said mockingly.

Furious, Ethelinda marched up to Vano and grabbed him by the collar. "How dare you?" She seethed.

"How dare I what," Vano said defiantly, "how dare I do what you didn't have the courage to do? You should be thanking me." Ethelinda glared at him, then shoved him away across the fire.

"You are disgusting," she said. Vano only laughed and shook his head.

"And you," he retorted, "are soft. Frankly, it's getting a little pathetic."

Ethelinda moved towards him, but started to get faint. Kezia rushed forward and grabbed her as she started to fall, looking into her face with concern. "Oh my..." she said, realization dawning on her face. "Ethelinda, are you with child?"

Ethelinda stood up straight, breathing heavily. "As a matter of fact, I am. Gaetan and I were going to tell his parents that we are expecting today, but this happened." She glared again at Vano and said, "You should be ashamed... your jealousy and hatred may not have harmed me, but they have hurt my child, who will never know his family now. You are pathetic, Vano... I should have left you to die a slave instead of saving your ass."

Vano's face became a mask of fury. He strode forward in two quick steps and grabbed Ethelinda by the arm. Kezia tried to step between them, but Vano brushed her aside. "You listen to me *cățea*. You saved me in the past, but I am much stronger now, and I will not be intimidated by a foolish whore like you. Watch how you speak to me, or I will do worse – not to you, but to that bastard... and his baby." Gaetan looked down at Ethelinda's belly. She tried to hide the fear on her face at Gaetan's threat, but he smiled maliciously. "That's right. I will put a curse on what matters most to you, and you can say goodbye to the precious baby you're so excited about." He looked away, pretending to be thinking. "I wonder, how will that bastard Frenchman handle losing his parents and his child, so close together. I imagine it would be more than his weak mind could handle."

Ethelinda could hear no more. She wrenched her arm away in distress, then hauled off and punched Vano as hard as she could in the face. He bent over double as blood began pouring from his nose. Ethelinda bent close to him and said, "You underestimate me, Vano. I love my husband and will do anything for my family, but my blood is still that of a Gypsy. If you threaten my family again, I will kill you slowly, painfully, and without a second thought." Her eyes burned with intense fury, and she said, "I will cut you open and make you watch as buzzards eat your entrails. I will feed them your eyeballs myself, one at a time. You have no idea what I am capable of, and I suggest you don't test me again." She straightened up, breathing heavily. She made eye contact with Kezia, who calmly walked over to where Vano was standing. She grabbed him by the shoulders and shoved her knee as hard as she could between his legs. As he bent over, howling in pain, another Gypsy woman walked up and kicked him in his side. He fell to the ground, curled up in pain, and suddenly, almost all of the Gypsy women were on him, kicking him in the back and in the sides.

Ethelinda smirked as he gasped for air, then said "Enough!" The Gypsy women, smiling with wicked pleasure, all backed away from his body as Ethelinda stepped forward. She looked at his crippled body, curled up and barely breathing. With extreme effort, Vano turned his bloodied face up and looked up at her. "You see, Vano, these are *my* people. I welcomed you into our tribe, but make no mistake – their loyalty lise with me. You had best watch how you tread... you can be removed as easily as you were welcomed in." With that, she turned away, dismissing him. A few women stepped forward and dragged his body away to clean and bandage his wounds.

Ethelinda stayed a while longer with the rest of her tribe. She sat with Kezia, just enjoying her presence and celebrating her pregnancy. After a time, she rose and said, "It is time for me to go. I must return to my husband. Losing his parents may be more than he can bear."

Kezia nodded. "I understand that cousin. Will you return soon?"

"I will be back, I just can't say when. I look forward to returning, and bringing my baby to meet its people."

"Until then, my dearest cousin." Kezia stood as well and embraced her cousin tightly. Ethelinda hugged and said goodbye to her harem, then disappeared back into the woods, going home to be with her husband.

CHAPTER TWENTY THREE

I n the months that followed, Gaetan became a shadow of his former self. He loved his wife and was excited for their baby, but depression at the loss of his parents constantly plagued him. On many occasions, Ethelinda would find him lying on their bed, just staring into space. At first, she would try to comfort him these times, making conversation and lying next to him to keep him company. She would go to the market and get his favorite foods and special treats, but nothing brought him out of his depression. Every time, he would say the same thing as he gave a sad smile, "Just give me time, *mon coeur*. I only need time."

Months passed, and Gaetan did improve. Though the sadness never quite left him, much of his natural goodness and peace returned to him. He and Ethelinda prepared for their coming child eagerly, both excited to be parents. One evening, they were in their home as usual, sitting at the table talking, when Ethelinda began to feel sharp, sudden pains. She gasped and held her stomach. Gaetan looked up and said, "What's wrong my dear?"

"I think the time into labor... run and get the doctor." Gaetan looked nervous, but ran to get the doctor, who lived not far away. Within fifteen minutes, he burst back in with the doctor. Ethelinda continued in labor, and Gaetan paced nervously as the doctor instructed her to keep pushing.

Forty five minutes later, sweaty and exhausted, Ethelinda held her baby in her arms. Gaetan kneeled by them and said, "My beautiful baby boy… and my beautiful wife." He kissed Ethelinda on top of the head.

Ethelinda smiled tiredly at Gaetan and said, "He is beautiful, absolutely perfect. He has your eyes, darling." Gaetan gently lifted the child from her arms.

"You are right… this child is perfect." Friar Angles entered the room, and Gaetan turned to him, "Ah, Friar, come see my son." The friar walked up and looked at the child in Gaetan's arms.

"Indeed, he is a beautiful boy," he said with a smile. "And what have you chosen to name him?"

"That is a good question," Ethelinda said with a small chuckle.

"Claude," Gaetan said definitively, "his name will be Claude." He looked at Ethelinda with tears in his eyes. "It was my father's middle name, and I want to honor him with this child. He and Maman would have loved him so."

Ethelinda looked at him with understanding and said, "I could think of nothing more appropriate. Friar Angles, meet Claude Frollo."

The friar smiled and said, "What a blessed boy. Little Claude will be raised in a home of love."

Gaetan sat close to Ethelinda, and she kissed her son on the forehead sweetly. "Yes. Claude will be like no other… he is our special child."

CHAPTER TWENTY FOUR

As a baby, I was cherished by my parents. I was their world, and they both doted on me. When I was one week old, my parents took me to be baptized by Friar Angles. Being a Gypsy, my mother did not understand the custom of baptism, but my father was insistent on me being raised in the Catholic faith, and she supported him in this decision. She dressed me in the finest clothes of pure white, and together, they took me to the Cathedral de Saint-Denis to be blessed by Father Renault. We arrived at the cathedral with Friar Angles and a few other friars. It was a small ceremony, with only a few of my father's friends and close family attending.

Father Renault began the ceremony. "We are here to welcome another new life into God's arms. This beautiful young life is loved by many, but none so much as Christ himself." He completed the ceremony, sprinkling holy water on me to wash away the sin into which all children are born. He then asked my parents, "And who will be the godparents of the child, and ensure that he is raised securely in the fear and admonition of Christ, and of the rites of our faith?"

Friar Angles stepped forward. "I will," he said with pride. Father Renault nodded with satisfaction and led him through the rites, officially designating him as my spiritual guardian. He then gave a final blessing over our family and gave the benediction over the service.

Afterward, everyone gathered outside, talking and laughing. After a while, Ethelinda noticed that Gaetan and Claude were not outside with everyone else. She stepped back inside the sanctuary and saw Gaetan sitting in a pew toward the front of the church, playing with the baby. "Well Claude," he said, "do you know that I grew up here? Yeah," he said as the baby giggled and smiled, clearly not understanding what he was saying. "This is your papa's home, Claude." He sighed, melancholy washing over his face as he looked up at the stained-glass windows. "This was my home. I was loved here... I belonged here, with my maman and papa. I wish they were still here, to know you and love you just like I do." The baby didn't understand but could sense that something was wrong with his father. He started to cry, but Gaetan lifted him up in his arms and shushed him, gently rocking him back and forth. "Do not worry Claude. Your papa is here, and I promise that I will always be here. With God as my witness, I will always take care of you, *mon fils*."

Ethelinda cleared her throat and walked forward to where Gaetan stood, holding me. "Are you all right, my love?"

"Oh yes – just having a little talk with my son," Gaetan said with a reassuring smile. "Here, take Claude outside... I just need a moment alone."

"Of course," Ethelinda said. She took the baby from Gaetan's arms. "I think I will take Claude for a little walk. We may be gone for a while, we will see you later."

"Until later," Gaetan said forgetfully, already lost in his own thoughts.

Ethelinda walked out of the church with me bundled in her arms. She looked around carefully, then walked toward the forest path that led to her harem. We arrived in no time at the harem, where only a few of the Gypsies were around. As she approached, Ethelinda called out a greeting. Kezia was among those waiting for the rest of the Gypsies to return, and she beamed brightly when she turned and saw Ethelinda. "Cousin!" she cried out excitedly, rushing over to give Ethelinda a hug. She looked at the baby wrapped in Ethelinda's arms and said, "And is this the child?"

"Indeed, this is my son." Ethelinda smiled at her cousin, then turned and faced everyone gathered. "Meet Claude Frollo."

The Gypsy women smiled, and Kezia said "Let us hold him, Linda. We will bless the child's life and ward off any evil spirits." Ethelinda handed her son to Kezia, and the Gypsies passed him around, chanting and holding a small ritual ceremony.

After the ritual, Ethelinda celebrated in the company of her people. After a time, she collected me, and we hurried back to Gaetan, who was oblivious to what had just happened. We went home, both of my parents smiling contentedly.

PART THREE

CHAPTER TWENTY FIVE

In a home of such love, you are likely wondering how I could have turned into the man that I am now – bitter, with a heart unable to love. Make no mistake, there were happy times in my infancy, but that changed quickly. It was really because, as much as they loved each other, there was still so much that my father couldn't know about my mother's life. She was a Gypsy, and she snuck off often to be with her people. My father, meanwhile, sunk into fits of depression often. His health suffered because of his depression, and he grew weaker all the time.

Still, in the first years of my life, I was a relatively happy child. We moved back to Saint-Denis, to a small home not far from where Gaetan grew up. My father loved me and took good care of me. He took me to mass every week, and though I was too young to understand what was happening, I still remember the singing and chanting of the priest and friars, the hymns and sermons. My father began to spend more time at the cathedral, cleaning the sanctuary and talking with Father Renault late into for hours. I would go with him sometimes, but more often, I was with my mother.

Ethelinda started going back to her harem more and more, and she would devise sneaky excuses and ways to bring me with her on these visits. She felt that I had a right to know her people and her culture, even if I was too young to understand them. She let my father raise me Catholic, but at the same time subverted his faith with her Gypsy ways. My father didn't really notice what she was doing, and I spent many nights sitting innocently at the Gypsy camp, too young to know that I was in a den of vipers. I actually enjoyed being there, sitting with Kezia, who was like an aunt to me, and watching all the bright colors and lively dances that took place. It was because of my mother and her harem that I started to learn both French and Romanian, the language they tossed back and forth so casually around the fire.

I faintly remember my nights spent around the harem. One instance that I remember vividly is from when I was two years old. Kezia had given me a tambourine, and I sat next to her, beating it and watching in fascination as the metal plates on the sides tinkled musically. Kezia watched me with a strange smile on her face, then leaned over and said quietly to me, "Watch, *puisor.*" She sprinkled a pinch of white dust on the tambourine. I barely noticed at first, but as I kept hitting the tambourine, I saw silver sparkles rise out of the dust, transforming into the silhouette of a beautiful dancer twirling and spinning around. Like a little fool, I laughed and smiled, amazed at the sight before me. "Well, Linda," Kezia said, turning to my mother, "it looks like the boy likes the tambourine. Shall we let him keep it? He may turn out to be a real gypsy yet."

"Of course he will," my mother said, picking me up. "If he's any blood of mine, he will know where he comes from. He will know our people." She kissed me on the cheek and gave the traditional call to the harem, "*Tigan Pentru Totdeauna*!" They all echoed the call. I was happy then, not understanding what sort of evil I was speaking. I look back now, wishing I had only known to stay far away.

CHAPTER TWENTY SIX

As time went on, my father had many more problems with his health. He got weaker and weaker, and spent a great deal of time in bed. Father Renault would come see him every day, and Friar Angles would also come visit frequently. I loved spending time with my father, but wasn't able to very often because of his poor health. Instead, I would spend days with my mother. It was not very pleasant going with Ethelinda – when she got around her people, it was like she became a totally different person, one who had no time for me. When I was very young, she would take me with her at night to commune with the rest of her harem, but this stopped after one terrible incident.

One night, when I was three years old, I sat around the fire with several of the gypsy women, enjoying music and listening to the people talk amongst themselves. I looked around, wondering where my mother was, but couldn't seem to find her anywhere. My mother had told me earlier to stay with Kezia, but I saw her over by a tree, talking and leaning against some man I had never seen before. Instead of staying there and sitting by myself, I went in search of my mother. I heard sounds coming from a tent on the far edge of camp, and I wandered over to it. In the shadows outside the tent, I saw the shape of two people who looked like they were rolling around, pulling on each other's clothes. Not knowing what I was looking at, I lifted the flap and went into the tent. "Mama?" I said. My mother was sweaty, kissing and being kissed by a strange man. At the time, I was scared and confused, and I stood, just staring, as the man continued kissing my mother's chest. When she heard me call her and saw me standing there, Ethelinda gasped and sat upright suddenly. She quickly grabbed her black shawl and covered her body. The man she was with also looked at me. He had a long scar across his face and dark, depthless eyes, and I was afraid when he gave me a slow grin. Ethelinda said nothing. She just stood and grabbed me by the arm, then marched me back to the camp quickly, practically dragging me when I couldn't walk as fast as her. She sat me down back at the fire, then stalked up to where Kezia was standing, still flirting with the other man.

Ethelinda grabbed Kezia by the arm, and they had a quiet conversation in Romanian. I didn't fully speak the language yet, but I could tell they were talking about me. I was embarrassed and felt guilty even though I didn't quite understand what I had done. I sat crying as they talked. Kezia nodded once, and my mother walked away, back to her strange tent and strange man.

Kezia came up to me and said, "No more wandering off *puisor*, your mother and I are too busy tonight to watch you. Can you be good for me tonight Claude?" I nodded silently and spent the night miserably sitting alone by the fire.

CHAPTER TWENTY SEVEN

Our family went on this way for a while: broken, just barely functioning. My mother, for all her ways, did love my father truly, and she did everything she could to keep him comfortable and make him happy. At times, she was the only one who he would talk to or let into his room – not even I could go in and see him. His health stabilized for a short time, and just when it seemed things might turn around, he contracted the Black Death. It had already wiped out so many across France, but still came as a shock when it touched our home. For our own safety, my mother and I had to leave the house to avoid the risk of infection. Friar Angles offered to let us stay with him, and we left soon after we got the news. The night before we left, Ethelinda snuck back into the room where Gaetan lay sick. She looked at him lying there, and tears welled in her eyes. She did not come any closer,, nut whispered from the door "Goodbye *mon coeur...* you will always be my heart." She took one last look at her husband, then silently crept back out of the room. I had never seen my mother as broken-hearted as she was when we left home with Friar Angles the next morning. She knew, even then, that she would never see my father again.

We received word one month later that my father had died. Ethelinda was broken by the news, and she went into deep mourning. She did not go anywhere for two full weeks, not even to be with her harem. I was also hurt at the loss of my father, but as a child of only five years old, I didn't truly grasp the finality of death. I kept thinking that my father was gone for a while, but that he would be back soon to play with me and hug me just like he always had. I didn't realize just how serious his death was until his funeral.

The day we laid my father to rest, my mother and I arrived early at the cathedral with Friar Angles. All bodies of plague victims were burnt to prevent the spread of infection, but we still got an empty casket for my father. Father Renault read the final rites for Gaetan, his voice breaking as he committed to the ground the young man who he had watched grow up. My mother was inconsolable, and cried for the whole service. I was scared – of my mother and all the crying people, of the dark and serious ceremony, and mostly of the thought that I would never see my papa again. At the end of the service, loud chiming rang from the bell tower. The brassy sound of the bells made my head ache, and I started crying. Ethelinda looked over and saw me crying, and as I looked up at her, I saw how deeply hurt she was. Her eyes were watery and bloodshot, and the tips of her nose and ears were all pink. She held my hand gently and laid me against her side. That was the closest I ever felt to my mother, as we sat in the cathedral, crying and thinking of my father, Gaetan.

When we left the cathedral, my mother and I returned with Friar Angles to his home. When we arrived, he asked my mother if she had a moment to speak with him. "Ethelinda," he began, "I know how much Gaetan meant to you. He was such a good man, truly blessed with a heart of kindness and charity. I loved him, and the least I could do is look out for his family. I know how hard things will be for you and Claude being alone, and I just want you to know that my home is always open. You can stay here as long as you need to."

My mother smiled, tears running down her face once more. "Thank you friar. Things will never be the same without Gaetan... he was the most special person I have ever known. He loved without judgment, always looking for the best in people. I didn't deserve him, and I will miss him dearly. Your kindness and support in a time like this mean so much Claude and me." She reached forward and hugged the friar, who hugged her back. "Do not worry about me, though, I do have family in the area: my harem.

I can go and be in mourning there. Without Gaetan, there is nothing to keep me here when I know my people are out there. I do have one request though. I would so appreciate it if Claude can stay with you and be raised up in the Catholic faith… it is what his father always wanted, and Claude could use more men, especially men of God, in his life."

"Of course, Ethelinda," the friar agreed. "I understand your desire to go back to your people. Claude can stay here – I will take care of him as if he is my own.." Ethelinda smiled and started to thank Friar Angles, but he stopped her with a word of advice. "Just be careful out there Ethelinda, you never know who you can really trust. Remember that the doors of the church are always open to you, and more importantly, that God's arms are always opened to you too." Ethelinda thanked the friar and hugged him once more.

CHAPTER TWENTY EIGHT

A year later, I was visiting with my mother and her harem. I had been spending most of my time at the church with Friar Angles, but still spent time with my mother occasionally. On this occasion, she had chosen to bring me to another celebration, with singing and dancing and even delicious foods. The man who I had seen before with my mother in the tent, I learned, was called Vano. He had been gone for quite some time, but had returned to the harem recently. He and my mother sat together, and she said to the gathered crowd of Gypsies, "I have big news to share with you all... I am with child – Vano's child." I was excited at the idea of a new baby brother or sister, but the people all looked shocked and a bit confused. After a few moments of uncomfortable silence, Kezia spoke. "Congratulations cousin, we are all very happy for you." The others soon followed suit, congratulating Ethelinda and Vano.

Even to me, though, their well wishes sounded forced, and I wondered why that was. I was still excited, though, and I said to my mother, "Wait until I tell Friar Angles and Father Renault! They will be so excited for us Mama!" Ethelinda leaned towards me with a stern look on her face and said, "Listen to me closely Claude: you are not to tell anyone outside of this circle about this baby."

"But why, Mama?" I pressed. "Isn't this good news?

Ethelinda lashed out and grabbed me by the collar, yanking me up close to her. She yelled at me, "*imparte asta la nimene, intelegi!*?" She shook my shoulders and asked me again in Romanian, "*intelegi?*" I nodded my head, my face turning red with shame, and whispered, "I understand." She pushed my away and shook her head, running her hand through her hair with exasperation. Vano looked at me with a smug smirk. "You shouldn't take your anger out on the kid," he said to my mother.

"I am not angry, he just needs to learn to stay in a child's place. I won't tolerate disrespect." She shook her head and changed the topic, dismissing me. My embarrassment turned to anger with my mother, and with Vano. I started to feel like she didn't love me, not really, and didn't care what happened to me.

As she continued her conversation, I slowly and quietly walked away from the group, hoping not to be noticed. When I got far enough away, I began to run as fast as I could away from that place. I ran and ran, not knowing where I was going. When I was too out of breath to continue, I slowed to a walk and looked around. I realized that I had come to the end of the path leading me back into town. I heard bells ringing from the tower of the cathedral, and I headed in that direction.

As I approached the sanctuary, I heard the priest and friars chanting the Confiteor. I stood behind one of the pillars just outside the doors, watching as Father Renault waved the thurible, smoke filling the air as they chanted. As I listened to the holy men, I felt relief and peace, as though God had given me a refuge away from my mother and her wickedness. I walked into the sanctuary and silently sat in the back where I couldn't be seen, enraptured by the holy ritual taking place before me. I closed my eyes and just listened, letting the sound fill me with comfort.

When the prayer was over, I heard footsteps coming in my direction. I opened my eyes and peeked around the corner to see who was coming. Friar Angles walked up the aisle with another monk, discussing preparations of the sanctuary. "You take care of the altar and make sure that it's all clean," he directed. "I will take care of the sanctuary." As Friar Angles spoke, he looked around the sanctuary and saw me peeking around the corner. We made eye contact, but he said nothing to me. Instead, he carried on his conversation with the other monk. Eventually, they finished talking, and the monk walked away, up towards the altar. Friar Angles stood until he was far gone, then said in a calm voice, "You can come out now, Claude." I stood and slowly walked over to Friar Angles, worried that I might be in trouble. As I approached, though, he gave me a kind smile that made me feel calm, knowing that I could trust him. "I'm surprised to see you here, son. Weren't you supposed to be with your mother today?"

I hesitated, trying to think of what to say without telling the friar about my mother. "Well, I was with her, but then I wanted to take a walk. Yeah, I went for a walk and they didn't notice, so I just came here when I heard the bells ringing. And then, I heard you all singing and I felt good, so I didn't want to leave again." I nodded, thinking in my young mind that this explanation made total sense. Friar Angles smiled knowingly. He patted me on the head. "Say no more my boy. I understand, and God understands your heart. Follow me, Claude."

Friar Angles began walking towards the front of the sanctuary, and I followed behind him. "Do you know what the word 'sanctuary' actually means, Claude?" He asked me. I shook my head, and he continued, "It is a safe place. A home where anyone can belong, where they can find shelter and comfort." We stopped walking when we got to the front of the sanctuary, and I looked up at the stained-glass windows, the images bathing the cathedral in light and color as the sun shone on them. Friar Angles looked over at me and said, "This is your home, and was the home of your father and his father before him. In this cathedral, Claude, you will always have sanctuary." He reached over and put his hand on my shoulder, and we both stood, looking up at the windows.

CHAPTER TWENTY NINE

O ver the next few months, I spent as much time as possible with Friar Angles, avoiding my mother and her harem. As she continued in her pregnancy, though, she started to get happy again, and she treated me better. I was with her when she gave birth, in the same tent where I had once seen her making love. The women helped her as she was in labor, and the others all waited outside, chanting and saying incantations for a healthy delivery. I waited outside for hours until, finally, we heard the baby cry. Excited, I hurried toward the tent to see my baby brother or sister, but couldn't get through the crowd already surrounding my mother and the baby. I squeezed my way through until I could see the baby in my mother's arms. To my surprise and confusion, though, the baby girl in my mother's arms did not look like any baby I had seen before. One of her arms was shorter than the other. The right side of her face was sunken, causing her left eye to be farther down than the right, and her nose to be twisted. As I stepped closer, I also saw that her little body looked bent, like her body had been broken. I was shocked, but somewhere in my mind, I also noticed that the baby had beautiful black hair. My mother looked at the baby in horror, and tears streamed down her face. Kezia, also crying, stepped forward and said, "Linda, clearly this baby has been born with a curse. You know what must be done."

"Yes," my mother said in a heavy voice, "I will handle it tonight." The women started filtering out of the tent, and Vano burst in to see his child. When he saw the deformed baby girl, his eyes filled with angry tears.

"What have you done to curse this pregnancy? How could this be? This is not my child." He looked once more at the baby with disgust, then turned and stalked out of the tent. Kezia hugged my mother, then she too turned and left the tent. I was alone with my mother and the baby. She sat looking at the little girl, crying silently.

I walked forward cautiously and looked closer at the baby. "Is this my baby sister, mama? Will she be alright?" My mother said nothing and only cried harder. I wanted her to feel better, so I said, "Do not cry Mama. Even if she's sick, we will love her, won't we? I will help you take care of my sister." My mother shook her head and said sadly, "Leave us please Claude, just *iesi afara.*" Not knowing what to do, I left the tent, full of hurt and sadness. I sat and cried. That was the quietest night I spent at the gypsy camp. Instead of the usual laughing, talking and singing, the people spoke in hushed tones and whispers. My mother and the baby didn't come out of the tent for hours.

Late that night, I could not sleep. I had stayed at the camp, hoping to see my mother and baby sister come out of the tent. I finally fell asleep, but woke when I heard footsteps crunching quietly through the leaves. I woke, and could barely see in the pitch black night. I could just make out my mother, dressed all in black, carrying the baby away from the camp. The baby was wrapped from head to foot in black rags and bundled tightly in my mother's arms. I said nothing, but followed at a safe distance to see where my mother was going. She headed down a path deeper into the woods, and I followed carefully. Eventually, she stopped at an old well in a small clearing. I hid behind a tree and watched as she carried the baby closer. She looked into the child's face one more time, then held her above the well. As she said some words quietly in Romanian, I realized in horror what she was about to do. Just before she let go of the baby, I ran out from my hiding place, crying out "Mama, stop!" My mother turned, startled and still holding the baby, who began to cry. I ran up to her and grabbed her skirt, begging for her not to do it. My mother callously kicked me back onto the ground, saying "I must kill this curse, it is the only way." I laid on the ground, unable to get up. She turned and dropped the crying baby down the well. I screamed and sobbed as my mother stood, looking into the well. After a minute had passed, she turned and walked towards me. She looked down with a cold, expressionless gaze and said, "It is finished. Get up Claude, it is time to go back." With that, she walked away, back in the direction of camp. I sat up, and stayed there, crying, late into the night. I was only seven years old, but that night, something in me changed. For the first time, I hated my mother. That act of cruelty was more than I could bear, and I vowed that I would never be like my mother and the rest of the cursed Gypsies.

PART FOUR

CHAPTER THIRTY

I spent less and less time around my mother and her people, instead choosing to spend my days in Saint-Denis, sitting in the cathedral for hours. I would go only occasionally to see my mother, but she never seemed to care if I was there or not. She went on about her life, going out and working with her harem, seducing men and stealing from them. When I was ten years old, she gave birth again, this time to a healthy baby boy. My little brother was named Jehan. A few short months after Jehan was born, my mother got sick with the Black Death. She died not long after that.

Friar Angles and Father Renault learned of her death and expected me to be in mourning, but were surprised to see how apathetic I was. In truth, I had stopped loving my mother long ago, and I knew that she barely cared for me. I felt that she reaped what she had sown, and that her death was just punishment for all of her sins. Still, I attended the gypsy "ceremony" for her death. They gathered around the body late at night, setting it on fire. As my mother burned, the savages chanted and sang in Romanian. I did not join in the barbaric ceremony, but watched from a safe distance. I stared into the fire, watching my mother's body burn before my eyes, and couldn't help but think that it was only fitting, as she would burn in hell for the rest of eternity anyway.

After the ritual, Kezia walked up to me as I sat in front of the fire, lost in my own thoughts. She touched me on the shoulder, startling me. "*Puisor*," she said, calling me a nickname I hadn't heard in years, "I have missed you – you spend so much time with your father's people. Your mother may be gone, Claude, but you are still one of us. You are welcome here anytime." I looked at her skeptically, and she said, "There is something I want you to have, so that you always remember where you come from." She reached into the satchel at her side and pulled out an old tambourine and a small black pouch. "You loved these when you were a baby, do you remember? Here," she said as she reached into the bag.

Kezia pulled out a small pinch of dusty white powder and sprinkled it over the tambourine, which she then started playing. As she beat rhythmically on the tambourine, the dust rose into a small pillar of smoke. I watched as a female silhouette formed in the smoke, dancing seductively. The image before me felt familiar and inviting, and this terrified me. I didn't want any part of the Gypsy witchcraft, but I knew it was still undeniably in my blood. In frustration, I reached forward and snatched the tambourine out of Kezia's hands. The image disappeared in a puff of smoke, and I stood, saying, "I remember no such thing. I am my father's son, not a Gypsy bastard. I wish I had never known you cursed witches, and I will never return to this wretched place." I dropped the tambourine to the ground and stood, looking defiantly at Kezia.

Instead of being angry, only sadness was in her eyes as she looked back up at me. "I see," she said as she stood. She picked up the tambourine and pouch once more. "Claude, there was a time when your mother tried to forget who she was. She married your father and thought she could live a normal life, like one of them. It took her time to realize that, no matter how hard she tried to fight, she would always be one of us – it was in her blood." She looked into my eyes and handed me the tambourine and powder again. "You may fight it all you want, Claude, but you will always be one of us – it's in your blood."

I looked at Kezia, my resolve wavering for just a moment. Finally, I said, "As far as I am concerned, you will all rot in hell. I wouldn't dare be associated with your wickedness. I will fight forever if I must, but I will never be one of you." With that, I turned and walked away from the camp

for the last time. I could feel Kezia's eyes on my back as I left, never to
return.

CHAPTER THIRTY ONE

From that day on, I dedicated my life wholly to the church and to the Catholic faith. I spent all of my time with Father Renault and Friar Angles, who taught me about the faith. I was a dedicated student, and soon Friar Angles began taking me with him on his trips to visit the ministries in other towns. One of the places that we visited most frequently was the Cathedral of Notre Dame. The priest there, Father Leonard, was a most righteous man. He imparted wisdom into me, and I was always eager to learn from him.

I became closer with Father Leonard, and he invited me to be a minister under him at Notre Dame when I was just sixteen years old. I was truly flattered, but declined. Friar Angles needed me, and I didn't feel at all prepared for such a big responsibility. Still, he told me that the doors of his church were open, and that I was always welcome.

The next year, Friar Angles and I were in town during the Notre Dame's grand Feast of Fools. I had never seen such a celebration, and I asked the friar, "What is this festival? I don't know what to expect."

"Well," he explained, "it is essentially a large festival. The *fête de fous* began as a religious ceremony, but it is now just an opportunity for the people in town to have a celebration. Everyone parties in the streets, and there is all kinds of food, music, singing and dancing."

"My goodness, that sounds exciting!" I replied eagerly. "I would love to go... with your permission course, sir."

Friar Angles chuckled. "Of course you many go, Claude. You are still a young man, and you need to experience life. I'm sure it will be great fun. As a matter of fact, I may stop by myself for a short time – if only for the food. It begins tomorrow. We will go together after morning mass, how does that sound to you?"

"That sounds excellent, thank you friar!" I smiled excitedly, eager for the next day's celebration.

The morning of the festival, I could scarcely contain my excitement. I sat through mass, but heard practically none of the father's words. I went through the motions of prayer, my mind on the afternoon's festivities. As I thought about it, I started to worry a bit, wondering about the Gypsies. This was exactly the kind of event that they would try to take advantage of. Happy people full of food and drink in large crowds would be paying no attention to their personal belongings – the perfect opportunity for the Gypsy people to slip through the crowd, looting and picking pockets. The very idea angered me, and I resolved to handle any Gypsy disruptions myself. Just turning them into the authorities wouldn't be enough. I would kill them myself if I had to. With that reassuring thought in mind, I was excited once more for the festival.

After mass, I went to the guest room where Friar Angles and I were staying to change my clothes. I chose a simple outfit, and after much deliberation, walked over to my small chest in the corner of the room. I unlocked it and pulled out two items: the tambourine and powder that Kezia had given me years ago. Nobody, not even Friar Angles, knew that I still had it, but the urge to use the wicked items was too strong for me to resist. I didn't use them, but kept them because I couldn't bear to throw them away. I looked at them for a moment, then tucked them back away in my chest, trying to forget.

As I locked the chest, I heard Friar Angles come into the room behind me. "Are you ready Claude? The festival is already underway." I stood, smiling, and said, "I certainly am! Let us be on our way."

As we walked outside, Friar Angles said in a tone of warning, "Now be careful Claude… it's easy to get lost in crowds like these. Stay close to me as much as possible."

"Friar," I said, laughing and rolling my eyes, "you don't need to worry. I think I can handle myself."

"Well, alright son. Just remember what I said and be careful." I promised that I would and made plans to meet the friar in two hours, then went my own way into the street.

CHAPTER THIRTY TWO

Just as the friar had said, the street was packed with people celebrating. It was more people than I had ever seen in one place! Women in brightly colored clothing talked and walked in the street, wandering up to vendors who called out *"Fruits et legumes frais! Épices exotiques! Beaux tissus!"* The vendors sold delicacies that I had only heard of, but never seen before that day. There were musicians on every corner playing beautiful songs, and children running around carrying the foods and treats that they were only allowed to have on these special days: *des bonbons, amandes épicées,* and *pain léger.* The busy, festive scene lightened my heart, and I walked around casually, taking in all the sights and sounds. As I wandered down one street, I heard a different sound, one that was much less welcome to my ears. It was the distinct sound of tambourines and traditional Romanian songs. I walked toward this familiar sound, and soon came across a group of gypsies singing and dancing in the street. I wanted to walk away, but was drawn by one Gypsy woman in particular . The woman didn't look like the rest of the Gypsy vagabonds. She was short, with clear gray eyes, tan skin, and straight, blonde hair that reminded me of clean sand on a beach. I could not take my eyes off her as she moved – the way she spun and swung her hips captivated me. She saw me in the crowd and our eyes locked. She smiled at me as she danced, and something about the confidence of her movements minded me of my mother. She continued looking at me, and I could not look away.

As the dance finished, the blood rushed up to my face. I stood there even as the Gypsies walked around, collecting francs from the crowd. The mysterious, beautiful dancer walked up to me and grinned, giving a small curtsy. I gave a sight bow in return and complimented her dance in Romanian. "*Spectacol minunat,*" I said with a slight smile. Her grin widened further, and she asked "*stii sa vorbesti romaneste?*"

"Yes," I replied, "my mother was a Gypsy, so I speak the language. May I just say, you are quite lovely." She blushed slightly, and I asked, "What is your name? I am Claude."

"I am Rosella, and it is a pleasure to meet you Claude. Would you care to walk with me?" She smiled seductively, and I agreed. We walked through the streets together for quite some time, flirting and talking. After a short time, it was clear that we were attracted to each other, and we started sneaking kisses from one another as we walked. I took her hand and led her down an alley. We kissed more and started breathing heavily, and I started undressing. She pulled her skirt off, and we had sex right there in the alley.

Afterward, we stood panting and breathing heavily. I smiled at her and said, "thank you for a fun time Rosella." I turned to walk away, but she stood in front of me. "Where do you think you're going asshole? Don't you know you have to pay me?"

"What are you talking about?" I said, realization dawning on me. "I should have known you were just another Gypsy whore... I can't believe I fell for your pathetic act. Get out of my way you Gypsy bitch." I shoved her roughly aside and walked away, but two big gypsy men emerged from the shadows. They looked at me and laughed, and one said in Romanian, "Not so fast."

Rosalie stood from where I had pushed her down and walked up to me with a smug smile. "Aww, did you think we were alone? Please. As if I would ever go with a pig like you without protection." Furious, I slapped her across the face. The two giant men grabbed me and pulled my arms back as hard as they could. My right shoulder popped out of the socket, and I screamed as fire tore through my arm. Rosalie walked up closer to my face, breathing heavily, and said, "You will pay for that. Give me what I am owed before you are hurt." In response, I spit in her face, then tried my best to kick her in the stomach. She backed away, glaring and wiping her face, and the two men started to beat me. Punches landed in my stomach and heavily on my face, and when I fell to the ground with a thud, their feet fell on my stomach and back. They kicked me until I thought my lungs would come out of my throat, and I could barely breathe. When I thought I would black out and surely meet death, Rosella said calmly, "I think he has had enough."

As I panted, every breath was agony to my aching lungs. I could not look up, but saw Rosella's shadow fall above me. She spoke with an icy venom in her voice. "You should have just paid me, Claude. Now you know better. Don't think that just because your mother was a Gypsy, you can get away with shit like this. You are a Frenchman dog, and you will be treated like one." She kicked me one last time in the stomach, and I collapsed on to the stone street once more. My head hit a stone, and as I passed out, I heard the Gypsies cackling as they ran away.

I was out cold for a short time, and as I came to, I sat up, wincing in pain. I reached up with my sleeve and felt the blood dripping from my nose. With much difficulty, I stood, realizing that I was supposed to have met Friar Angles some time ago. I walked slowly and painfully back towards our meeting place, mentally chiding myself for falling into the gypsy trap. I had such a righteous indignation, and I knew the Gypsies were wicked, yet still allowed myself to be seduced like a damn fool. Guilt and shame weighed heavily on me, and I determined even more to never be taken in by the Gypsy deceivers again.

When I finally made it back to our meeting place, I saw the friar waiting and pacing nervously. He looked over and saw me approaching. As he took in my bloodied and disheveled appearance, Friar Angles came rushing up to meet me. "Claude, what terrible thing has happened? How did you come to look like this?" He examined my face as he waited for my answer, his face awash with concern. I quickly conjured up a lie; I was a minister in training, and the truth could be detrimental to my training. "Friar," I began, "you were right. I should never have ventured out by myself. I got lost, and some Gypsy thieves spotted me. They must have known how inexperienced I was. They cornered me in and alley and demanded that I give them all my money. I of course gave it to them, but they beat me up anyway."

Friar Angles bought my story completely. He asked a few questions about where this happened and why there was nobody around who could help, but I quickly came up with answers. Eventually he stopped asking and said "Oh Claude, I am so sorry this happened. Do not worry son, you are safe now. Come inside, let me take care of you." We went inside, where the friar cleaned me up. I could tell he still had questions about what happened, but he didn't ask, and we spoke no more of it.

CHAPTER THIRTY THREE

Years passed, and I refocused my devotion to the Catholic faith. I was dedicated not just in ministry, but in service to the community and to the prayer outreach sessions that we offered. Father Renault got older and weaker as the years passed, but still served faithfully in the Cathedral of Saint-Denis. While I worked under him, he would tell me all sorts of stories about my father growing up, and how he became a fine, righteous man. I didn't remember much about my father, and I loved hearing Father Renault's stories. He even spoke of my mother, and how he met her when she came looking for sanctuary. It surprised me to hear this, and I wished I could have known my mother then, before she became so bitter and wicked.

Sadly, Father Renault passed away when I was nineteen years old. I mourned the loss of this great man with all of the congregation of Saint-Denis. He was loved by all, and he encouraged me to stay on the path of righteousness. I think even my mother would have owed him a debt of gratitude for the kindness he showed to her so many years ago, saving her from the death she rightfully deserved. As long as I live, I will not forget his welcoming spirit and dedication to the faith.

After Father Renault's passing, Friar Angles and I began spending more and more time in the Cathedral of Notre Dame. After ensuring that the next priest in line took over and effectively shepherded the flock at Saint-Denis, we moved to Paris and began serving in Notre Dame under

Father Leonard. I trained and learned under the priest, and in a short time, I was elevated to the position of minister. Father Leo trained me well, and I continued to grow under the tutelage of him and Friar Angles.

Soon, I started to feel that God was calling me to be more than just a deacon – I wanted to become a priest in a church of my own. One day, I approached Father Leonard to ask him if I could begin training to be a candidate for priesthood. When I told him how I felt, Father Leonard hesitated, and I started to get nervous. "Well, son," he said delicately, "this is not a decision that can be made lightly. Are you sure this is what the Lord is speaking to you?"

"Yes sir," I responded confidently. "I am being called to something much greater. If you give me the opportunity, I will prove myself."

"I see. Claude, I will need to discuss this with my archdeacons and monks. I will let you know what we decide." I thanked Father Leonard, then kissed his ring and left the room.

Later, the priest met with the other leaders to discuss my request to become a candidate for the priesthood. Friar Angles was in the meeting, and he listened as all the other men voiced their opinions both for and against me as a candidate. Father Leonard looked over at him and said, "Joseph, you are Claude's godfather, and you know him better than anyone here. What are your thoughts on the matter?"

Friar Angles looked at the priest in contemplation, then spoke. "Father, you and I both know Claude's heart. There is no doubt in my mind that he is dedicated to his faith and to serving the people of God." He hesitated, then continued, "At the same time, there is a side to Claude that I fear may hinder his ministry as a priest. He has had confrontations with the Gypsy people – just a few years back, he was in a confrontation with some Gypsy men at the *fête des fous*. His mother was a Gypsy, and I fear his upbringing has left him scarred when it comes to those people. He cannot serve as a priest unless he can learn to let go of the bitterness and forgive those people, for they are still souls who need us for sanctuary, and to bring them to salvation."

"That is very interesting," said Father Leonard, "and problematic indeed. I propose that we do not offer Claude candidacy yet, but monitor him closely when he ministers to the people. We will see then how he interacts with these Gypsy people, and will know how to respond from there." The church leaders all agreed, and a decision was made. When Friar Angles came home that evening, I looked to him eagerly to see if a decision had been made. His expression was inscrutable, however, and as I looked at him suspiciously, he told me that I would need to go meet with Father Leonard in the morning, and would say nothing more.

When I spoke with Father Leonard the next morning, he explained that they had decided not to recommend me for the priesthood. He said that I needed to spend more time in ministry before moving into something so serious. I was upset, but understood his reasoning.

CHAPTER THIRTY FOUR

At mass the following week, I was serving with the other ministers, getting ready before service began, when a family of gypsies walked into the sanctuary. My eyes narrowed, and I thought to myself, what in God's name are those filthy vagabonds doing here? Friar angles was watching my response, and he walked up to me and put his hand on my shoulder. I was startled, but tore my gaze away from the filthy people as he began to speak. "Claude, is everything alright?" I quickly pasted a fake smile on my face and said "Oh yes, everything is quite fine! I see we have some... guests amongst us today." I looked over at the Gypsy family, and the friar followed my gaze. "Ah yes, the Curzin family. They are in desperate need, Claude, so we welcomed them into the church. Come, I will introduce you."

Friar Angles took me by the arm and started walking to where the family was sitting. They were a young family, a husband and wife with two daughters, about three and five years old. I felt sorry for the children, knowing that they would grow to be pathetic whores, just like all Gypsy women... just like my mother. I could tell that the parents' poor, seeking refuge act was fake, and it took all my willpower not to strangle them where they sat. I just barely kept my composure. Seeing how Friar Angles was watching me, I kept the fake smile glued to my face and walked with him up to the family. When we arrived, the friar introduced me to the parents. I gave a short bow, but then excused myself and walked away before I lost my composure. Many of the leaders watched me carefully after that, putting me in positions where I would have no choice but to deal with the Gypsies. Every time I was left alone with them, though, I would find ways to get revenge. When I thought no one saw me, I would ignore their prayer requests and pleas for sanctuary. When I rode on my horse and saw Gypsy children, I would purposely ride up as if to trample them underfoot, smiling as they scattered.

I thought I did these things in secret, but Friar Angles, Father Leonard, and many of the other monks, deacons, and ministers watched me with a growing concern. After some time, I was called into a meeting with the leaders to discuss my progress in the ministry. "Minister Frollo," Father Leonard began, "We can all see that you have a desire to live for and serve God faithfully. We appreciate your dedication to the service."

"However," Friar Angles said, leaning forward to look into my face, "we are worried about the way you interact with some people who come seeking sanctuary and refuge – particularly, the Gypsy people."

I tried to cover my concern with an innocent smile. "What do you mean by that, sir? I am sure I don't understand."

"Well, Claude, we have seen you on several occasions treat the Gypsy people with malice and unnecessary cruelty. These people come here, seeking sanctuary and salvation, and they are turned back to the street because of your behavior. We cannot allow this to continue," said Father Leonard regretfully.

I shook my head, already preparing to deny the priest's statements, but Friar Laurence stopped me. "Don't try to deny it, Claude. I know that you have been through a great deal with the Gypsies, and that you have suffered because of them. Please, though, don't let your anger with a few poison you against a whole population of people – people who need salvation, just like you and me." I looked at him with disbelief and anger, and he continued speaking. I know it doesn't seem possible, but you must find it in your heart to forgive, Claude. Forgive and move forward, or you cannot do what God is calling you to."

I stood up suddenly, my chair crashing backwards. I tried to control my anger, clenching my fists into balls tightly. Through gritted teeth, I excused myself and walked out of the room, slamming the door behind me.

CHAPTER THIRTY FIVE

Now, many years later, I stand in the bell tower of the Cathedral, thinking back on the many years that I came through. I often came up here over the years to spend time alone, thinking and watching the city move below.

Friar Angles continued for many years to try changing my heart and mind about the Gypsies, but to no effect. I continued to serve faithfully in the church, but was strictly against my mother's people. Friar Angles died of fever not long ago, but his words still echo in my heart. I want to forgive and move forwards, but know that there is no chance of that. I am forever divided in two – desiring to be closer to the Lord, but unable to let go of the darkness that keeps me from him. I am both my mother and father's child: a holy man of France, but with the dark spirit of the Gypsy within me.

As much as I bury myself in hatred and resentment, there is a part of me that knows Kezia's words, spoken so many years ago, were right: I have the blood of a Gypsy. I still pull out my tambourine at times, its ribbons old and frayed, and conjure up the image of the dancing woman. I cry as I watch it: alluring, beautiful, and wicked, just like my mother. What I don't tell anyone, and scarcely confess even in my own mind, is that as much as I hate the Gypsies, I hate myself even more for being unable to free myself, to completely sever my tie with them.

And so it is. I am a man blessed and cursed, unable to reconcile the two sides of my identity. For now, I will focus my resolve on destroying the cursed Gypsies that run rampant in my city. No matter what, there will never be a story about me caring for any kind of Gypsy. I have hardened my heart. This, readers, is how I became Claude Frollo.